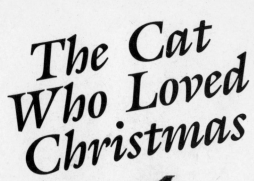

The Cat Who Loved Christmas

and other winter tales

Edited by Caren S. Neile

Contents

The Magic
of Cats

*W*e probably don't have to sell YOU on cats. Millions of people are already hooked on these uncanny creatures of mystery and charm, fluid grace and childlike mischief.

We have made cats our favorite domestic pet. If some of you need proof, take a stroll down the pet food aisle at your local supermarket or through the novelty section of any pet store. In the United States alone, cat lovers spend an amazing $500 million on their pets every year! And that *doesn't* include visits to the vet.

Wander into your local bookstore and look at the number of cat titles lining the shelves. Books and magazines about cats and cat people are a booming business.

Back by popular demand in a second printing, this charming little book, first published in 1994, makes an ideal stocking stuffer for any pet lover. It celebrates the cat in all her glory, whether she's matchmaking *(A Buddy for Christmas)* or jealous *(The Cat Who Went North)*. Some of the tales offer a fascinating cat's eye view of our world – *One of Our Pussycats is Missing* is a good example, as well as the title story *The Cat Who Loved Christmas*. Several are deeply moving, particularly the delightful love stories, *Pumpkin's Gift* and *A Collar for Chocolate*. There's even a story especially for the kids.

Each of these delightful tales will remind you why so many people feel the way we do about cats and kittens. Every cat owner feels that to be buddies with a cat is a truly unique, precious experience.

Open this book to any page – and feel the magic!

The Cat Who Loved Christmas

By PAUL CHRISTENSEN

I'm one of your run-of-the-mill cats, an orange half-Persian. My Persian half is kind of pretty, all fluff and fur, and I've been known to wear the occasional pink ribbon around my neck. My other half is well...whatever.

My father was any one of a number of tomcats from the back alleys. I'm sorry to say my mother had no taste when it came to male companions. She slunk away from home one night to hang out among the empty stretches of Venango Avenue. Propped up against a convenient fence, she batted her eyes at passing strangers. It pains me to think that I'm the result of that sort of hasty encounter. But there it is; like everyone else, I'm stuck with my own peculiar history. Call it fate.

I found myself in a pretty comfortable life with a

nice family out in the suburbs. I hung around on windowsills, and took long, leisurely naps on the sofa. Which is what we cats are famous for, of course.

I didn't much mind being petted by Susie, the little girl who looked after me. She fussed over me and liked to dress me up in doll clothes and put me into a basket with a satin pillow.

I would put up with it as long as I could. But there always came a time when I couldn't take any more and jumped out of the basket. Then she'd chase me down to get her clothes back.

The boy was older and had a mean streak. His name was Tommy, but I never called him that. I would greet him with a deep meow – nothing too personal. It was our little understanding, since we didn't get along too well.

When no one was around, the boy would take me by the neck and dangle me over the toilet while he flushed it. I knew he wouldn't drown me, but the experience was scary. I usually had to reach up and scratch him to get down.

It was with the big people I got on with the best. They had a routine for everything. It wasn't all roses, of course. I was cleaned once a week with a comb and dusted with flea powder. I wore a collar soaked in flea poison. That gave me the heebie jeebies. I had my ears poked with a Q-tip. My cat box wasn't cleaned too often, but when it was, it was sprinkled with an odor killer that took away a lot of the pleasure of rooting around in the gravel.

Otherwise, I pretty much had the run of the place. I got a fairly good meal of wet food in the evening and some dry stuff in the morning.

It seemed like that calm existence would go on forever until a few days before one particular Christmas.

I should tell you that Christmas has always been my favorite day of the year. For one thing, I was usually allowed to romp around under the tree and bat the shiny gold balls around. I also got a good share of tasty treats like sugar cookies and fruitcake. And then, at the opening of the gifts, there was always a catnip mouse.

Ah, the taste of catnip, that sweetest of sensations, would send me into the most delightful daydreams of peace on earth and goodwill toward – absolutely everything. Yes, I really did look forward to Christmas.

But on that particular December 22nd, my world turned upside down.

I was bored that afternoon – very bored. I caught myself yawning over a yawn, and sleeping so much I forgot what day it was. I thought, if I sleep anymore, I'll never wake up!

No one was home, so I got up from my basket on the windowsill, looking, I'll admit it, for some mischief. Well, I found it all right. You see, there was a key on the dresser in the boy's room. A big, shiny one on the edge of the dresser, next to his whistle and penknife. I think it was for his bicycle lock.

The key rattled when I pushed it with my paw. It moved so easily, it made me feel like a giant. How I loved that key! I slid it closer and closer to the edge of the dresser.

Suddenly, it fell to the floor. Oh, I was having a grand old time! I hopped down and pushed the key some more, under the dresser among the socks and dust. After a while I pushed it under a sock and couldn't get it out no matter how I tried. By then I was tired again, so I lay down, half under the dresser, and went to sleep.

> ❝ *Suddenly, it fell to the floor. Oh, I was having a grand old time!* ❞

When I woke up, I found the boy storming around the room looking for something. I had an idea what it was, too – that beautiful key. When his eyes at last fell on me, there was lightning in them. He couldn't see the key, but he knew I had something to do with it being missing, all right. Without a word, he lunged for me. I dodged so fast that he hit his head with a thud on the dresser drawer.

Growling now, he crawled around the floor in pursuit. He was very fast. But I was so scared that I jumped clear over his head and out the door, scratched for footing and got down the hall into the den, where I hid behind the couch. Right on my tail, so to speak, he was already pulling the couch away. I sprang at his hand, and I gave him a serious claw job. Then I raced up the hall and out the screen door just as the big people were coming in.

In tears, he showed them his big, bleeding hand. Boy, that made them mad. I saw Dad looking out the window, his face red and scowling. He looked like he wanted to kill me. Mom got bandages and ointment and said a lot of soft, comforting things to the boy, who sniffled and wiped his nose with his fist.

Then he looked up with that little boy stare of his, his eyes red and shining and mad, and said the words that every cat dreads: "I want a dog!"

Mom and Dad kind of cooed a bit and shuffled around, their faces breaking into secret smiles. Something was definitely up. So, I thought, they're *getting* a dog!

Oh, I've seen it before around this time of year, how they keep something hidden and then bring it down late at night and put it under the tree. Sometimes it's a bike or a baseball mitt or even a doll. But this time it would be a puppy – some goofy, drooling mutt chewing on the electric wires while everyone came down in pajamas oohing and aahing and begging to pet it. They would cuddle it and call it Mikey or Spikey or some loathsome name like that.

I, of course, would be left alone – until the little monster took after me with his teeth bared, that is. I would be out of the picture, done for, an old used-up toy no one wanted to play with anymore.

They would forget about me, not clean my box, not comb me, not change my collar. I would sit around scratching my fleas and have to hunt around in my litter box for a clean space. The dog would eat all my wet food and scatter the dry stuff around

11

the floor. I would smell his breath everywhere and find his hair wherever I went.

Life would be impossible! It was time for a change anyway, I told myself. All this sitting around purring on the couch was doing me no good at all. I couldn't spend my entire life being such a lump. Surely, there was some tough hunk of cat under all this silly fur. I had seen the movie *Born Free* dozens of times. I just KNEW I could be a lion if given half a chance. If I got mad, really roaring mad at the boy, why, I could box him into a corner any day. I was tough.

Besides, I couldn't stand the thought of playing second fiddle to a mutt. We cats have our pride, you know.

It was definitely time to leave.

The problem was I really didn't want to go. I hated the streets. I hated cold nights and lonely days. Hiding from strangers. Dodging stones and clods of earth thrown at me by wicked boys and skinny old men.

I'd heard horror stories about people shooting cats, or breaking their backs with a rake, or sicking dogs on them for no reason. I knew there were men driving around in big green trucks looking for stray cats. They grabbed them with a net and tossed them into the truck. Then they locked them up at the pound. No one wanted to adopt an adult stray, sitting there all battered and scarred in a tank full of homeless animals.

But I had no choice. My mother was out there living her life somewhere, after all. If she could make it, so could I.

I crept across the lawn, breathing in the scent of the tall, sweet grass one last time. At the curb, I paused to looked over my shoulder at the big, white house. When I heard a sad, strangled mew, it took me a couple of seconds to realize it had come from me. Then I hit the streets.

*T*he first night, I settled down in an old refrigerator shell I'd found tilted on its side on the edge of a landfill. I spotted a black tom with a mouse in his teeth sneaking into a bordering field. He kept looking back, then he dropped the little mouse and ate it. The tom was tough, a real cool customer with whiskers sharp as wires who wanted no company out there in the wasteland. When he caught my eye, he reared back, gave a low growl, arched and stiffened, and then began to flex his claws in and out.

In cat language, you have to understand, that's not exactly a friendly greeting. I retreated a few yards and waited. The big guy finished his meal, licked himself clean and went on his way. I wondered how long it would be before he'd come around to my temporary refrigerator lodgings. For all I knew, it was his bachelor pad. There were some leaves and sticks there to make a sort of bed, and a few chicken bones someone had gnawed on earlier.

I brought the leaves down around me and cuddled up as best I could. It was cold, and all night long there were ticking noises, and little feet moving around, and noses poking in to take a sniff. I feared for my life.

In the morning, the black cat was back, growling and demanding my space. It was his bed, sure enough. I made a run for it. Now I was out in the world again, with those men in the green trucks on the lookout for strays like me. Whenever traffic went by, I kept to the shadows and ran behind trees.

Little boys chased me from their yards, and a man yelled "SCAT!" and stamped his feet. I bounded off into a hedge.

Just when I was feeling really sorry for myself, I found some dry food in a bowl on a kitchen step. Starved, I ate it all. When at last I lifted my head, I noticed a kitten watching me from behind the screen door, all big eyes and pointy ears. Kind of cute, actually. Reminded me of myself when I was young. I said "Hello" and licked myself. He licked himself and stared back, copying everything I did.

Suddenly, a big, gruesome dog came up behind him and began to slobber and growl. I backed away up the street.

That afternoon, a cold, dark wind roared through the city. Women took their laundry off the clotheslines and shut all the windows. A newspaper careened down the sidewalk and curled around a lamppost.

I quickly learned that living on my own meant eating what I could find and sleeping wherever it looked halfway safe. I trusted no one, though one little girl stooped down to pet me. She said silly stuff to me, giggling and sighing until her mom dragged her away. That was the only friendliness I found that day. The rest of the time I spent running between hiding places or creeping around in tall, leafy hedges.

Inside one hedge I found a spider, a large silver and black thing with long claws, hanging in a loose web dotted with flies and bits of moth wing. She seemed fat and happy, dozing the afternoon away. As I sniffed around, however, she woke up and gave me one of those looks that tells you to move on.

A vast park lay ahead of me, the kind where men hit balls with shiny sticks and ride little cars. I thought I'd go in and have a stroll, and then find a bush where I could take a snooze.

I made it as far as the big sand trap and was about to use the bathroom when a voice behind me yelled so loud I jumped about a foot into the air. It was a man with a stick, and he was bright red in the face. He threw sand at me – got me in the eye – and I staggered and fell. I jumped again and ran, but right into his legs. In seconds, he had me by the tail and swung me over his head into a bush.

I think I broke something when I landed. Or twisted my leg, anyway. Whatever it was, I couldn't quite walk. My leg swelled and was soon numb. I licked it and even bit it where it hurt. After a while, the pain eased off.

It was then that I suddenly realized I wasn't alone. A face was staring at me from the branches. It was a little boy, and he was grinning down at me. He was saying something to the man, who came close. The guy got mad again and beat the bushes with his stick, but I couldn't move. I curled up and hissed, my last defense. Lucky for me, they moved on. I cried myself to sleep, but my ears were up the whole time.

That night I found no more food. Doors were shut tight, gates closed. People were staying inside because of the weather. The howling wind signaled the approaching winter night.

Despite my hunger and cold, I was enchanted by the brisk night. I saw snowflakes in the warm glow of the street light, little crystals drifting around like cotton balls. It was lovely, like the soft white powder they spray on Christmas trees. And the houses! All of them were lit with colored lights, and inside each house a beautiful tree was loaded with silvery balls and strings of tinsel and pretty trinkets.

> **❝ *I cried myself to sleep, but my ears were up the whole time.* ❞**

Through the windows, I could see people appear and disappear with trays of cookies and mugs of steaming cocoa. There was music in the air, as well. I passed a group of carolers muffled in scarves and hats.

Oh, but it was so cold. My feet stung with each step I took on the icy sidewalk. It had frozen into a white, slippery path.

Then, just as I wondered how long I'd be able to make it alone, an incredible thing happened.

I saw my mother. I could hardly believe it. She looked beautiful, her gray coat big and fluffy, her tail wonderfully plumed. Just when I needed her most, here she was!

She was darting along with a big alley cat, a powerful, scarred tom. Boy, did he look mean. When he saw me, he lowered his head as if to fight. I slunk back into the shadows, and he moved on.

I called to her, but, strangely, only a pathetic little mew came out. I wanted to cry out her name, or chase after her, but the tom kept looking back to see if I'd follow. I wouldn't. I sat down on a cold rock and began to knead my paws into the snow, hoping, somehow, for milk and warmth. I was so lonely and afraid.

Come back, Mom!

But she was gone, and my paws were wet and nearly frost-bitten from the snow. I shivered. For the first time in my life, I felt true terror.

I didn't know where home was anymore. It was back down a hundred crisscrossing streets, on the far side of a park or maybe two parks, I forgot which. It was some place where the traffic lights hung down over a corner, where big oak trees spread out their branches. But here there were no trees, only apartment houses – tall, gray buildings with rows of cars parked along the streets. And no one was outside, absolutely no one.

I found another alley, the kind my mother liked to hang out in. There was a big trash barrel next to a restaurant door and, stumbling a bit because of my sore leg, I climbed in. I could smell cooking odors pouring through the exhaust fan. It smelled like fish and potatoes. I breathed in the scent of spaghetti and vegetable beef soup – the sort of stuff my family ate.

It smelled delicious. My belly thumped, and my heart beat crazily. I could tell I was getting weak. The cold went right through me. Just then I caught my reflection in a shiny tin can: matted fur, dirty patches on my white face, a whisker missing. I looked old and tired. I looked half dead!

I didn't want to wash anymore; my whole body tasted of oil and soot and dirt. I couldn't bring myself to lick such matted hair. It was full of burrs. Oh, for a comb and a warm bath and a soft pillow to lie on! How I missed my home and all the love I'd lost. I wondered if anyone missed me. Or were they just thinking about their new dog? For all I know, they hadn't even noticed I was gone.

I suppose I slept. What woke me was the warm, thick weight of soup being poured over me. It covered me from head to paw. Then the lid went over the barrel! I was trapped. I was so sick I truly believed I was going to die, on Christmas Eve, of all days. The gooey stuff stuck to me, thickening as it cooled. It was like a suit of Jell-O. I retched.

> *'I was trapped. I was so sick I truly believed I was going to die on Christmas Eve...'*

I noticed a huge gray rat staring at me with beady little eyes. He crept toward me, his razor sharp teeth moving. I screamed, backed up, arched my back and got ready to kill, if need be. The rat stopped and began to slop up all the garbage. I crept back into a corner and waited for morning.

Suddenly the can rumbled and lifted up, then turned over, and the rat and I and a ton of garbage spilled into the cold, wet bottom of a garbage truck. I jumped high in the air, snagged my claws into a man's overalls, thrust my way over his shoulder as he batted at me with his gloved hands, and managed to pull his cap off before reaching the ground and springing into the cellar of the restaurant.

Staking out a corner in the dark, I could smell other animals there. It was a dreadful place, full of tall drums and dirt. There were rats and mice and other cats scurrying all over the place.

I jumped onto a high shelf to defend myself. And there, staring right into my face, was Mom. Beside her stood that mean black cat who had scowled at me.

Mom sniffed me all over and even licked a burr off my head. I curled up under her and smelled her warm belly, her large comforting paws. She purred and looked all over to see if I were hurt. Oh, I was, I told her; my leg was broken.

"No, it isn't," growled the old tom.

How did he know, I wondered. His fur smelled of the wild, and his breath stank of tuna. Each time he burped, I cringed. When he'd sniffed me up and down and seemed satisfied that I was all right, he whispered something to Mom.

She looked down at me with those soft gray eyes of hers and smiled. In a low monotone, she said, "This is your dad."

I gulped. That big, ugly thing! My FATHER? Oh, that was too shocking. He was filthy, and his fur was bitten out in huge clumps, or scratched out, maybe. He had huge, meaty haunches and mean-looking, spiky claws that could kill a ten-pound rat in a single swipe. His fangs were yellow and nicked, and his whiskers were as crooked as an old car antennae. He was the ugliest cat I had ever seen.

"You should be proud of him," Mom said, reading my thoughts. "You have his abilities or else you wouldn't have survived out here."

OK, I thought. I was pretty good, after all. Not quite a lion, but I had outsmarted quite a few enemies. But somehow that didn't make me less scared.

"Could I stay with you?" I asked.

Mom looked at my dad, and they seemed to say no, without actually saying the word. I just read it in their look. They had enough trouble living on their own. I was OK alone so far, but I guess they didn't consider me that sharp a lookout. I would be a burden to them.

One thing was certain: They had both become very smart and tough by living on their own. They knew the world far better than I did, maybe more than I ever would. I was still a plain old domesticated cat, no matter what I did. Horrible word, 'domesticated'. As if I wore little earrings and a powder blue muff and drank tea in the afternoon.

They backed away after a little while, and Mom said to take care. Silently, they leapt to the ground and went off, the old tom never letting down his guard. Nobody challenged them.

When they were gone, the scurrying started up again. There was some sort of fight over food scraps, and I think the rats won, though it was too dark to see. I slept, or rather napped, until I heard the basement window slam shut. Smelling danger, I slunk back into a pile of tomato cans.

*T*he lights went on and footsteps rang on the wooden stairs. A man came down with a huge stick attached to a floppy net. He swung it at various cats, who dodged and dove into the other rooms.

He was about to turn and go when he spotted me on the shelf. He leapt down, passed the net over me several times and, just as I was leaping away, caught me on one swing of the stick. I squirmed like a fish on a hook but in vain. He carried me up the stairs and out to his truck and tossed me rudely into a big metal cage. Off we went, with a few other mangy-looking cats cowering in corners.

So I was taken to the local animal pound. In that prison cell, we all curled up tight as little balls to keep ourselves warm. It was cold and wet. The snow had fallen hard that night and now drifted into the cages, which were open to the weather.

The place reeked, and food, very bad food, stale and dry and hard to bite, lay in little dirty bowls. Rainwater pooled in the middle of our cage, and cats crept up to lick it, but it was sour and evil-smelling. I felt like my heart was breaking.

It was Christmas Eve. I heard one of the guards say it to a woman who had come to find her cat. She looked us over and wrinkled her nose at the smell. She went away again. A man came over and pointed out two or three of the sickest cats and they were taken away.

After a while more cats came in, scooted out of the truck into our cage. One was a huge female with a kind face, heavy fur on her head and sides. She sat down calmly beside me and licked her paws. I must have been staring at her, because she looked up at me and smiled.

She said it would be OK for me, I was still young enough to be adopted.

"What about you?" I asked.

"Oh, I'll make out," she said. "I always have." And she continued her licking as if she owned the place.

Once more, I cried myself to sleep. It was Christmas Eve, and I knew my house smelled of cookies and mint and the sweet pine of the tree, with the lights gently flickering and music jingling from the stereo.

The Mom and Dad would be upstairs wrapping presents. I loved to sneak up and watch them work. All the secret toys and gifts were sitting on the bed unwrapped, and I could see what everyone was getting. The kids didn't know a thing; they were sitting downstairs watching movies, eating popcorn and drinking mugs of steaming hot cider.

The snow would be gently falling outside. The Mom would give the Dad a kiss and they'd run down to hand out cookies to the carolers.

How I missed them now, even Tommy. He wasn't so bad after all. I wished I could crawl into his lap and lick his fingers. What I would have given for the stroke of a comb across my fur, or a hand to touch me, to show me love!

But here I sat, a beat-up alley cat. Who knew how much longer I could hang on? My luck had run out. I could only dream of the soft night ahead, the swirl of lights, the laughter and singing. Of my beloved Christmas.

Just then, the cage door creaked open and the man in the boots came in. I didn't look up. I hoped he would pass me by. Please, I said, not today. Let me make it until Christmas.

But his grubby fingers dug into my sides, and I was pulled up into the air. I stiffened and bared my claws, but he had me by the waist. He carried me into a warm room and plunked me down on a table, his hand pinching my neck.

In dread, I looked up to meet my fate head-on.

And there they were! Mom, Dad, Tommy and little Susie!

Susie was crying and laughing and reaching for me, but Mom stopped her. I had to be bathed first, she said firmly, but she gave me a soft look. She patted my head, and the guard handed me to Dad, who wrapped me in a warm towel.

They carried me to the car, and we drove straight home. I was put in a bowl on the kitchen table, a special privilege, and washed in warm, sudsy water. Then I was combed out, powdered, and given a new collar. When I caught my reflection in a coffee pot, I was amazed. I looked beautiful again!

That night, I played under the tree. I looked up at myself in the big silver ball that hung just inches above my head.

And there was my family gathered around me, looking down with big smiles. Even Tommy said kind things. I curled up and slept beside my catnip ball. It was still wrapped up, but I knew what it was from the smell, of course.

And best of all, there was no puppy! The Mom and the Dad had decided that one cat — yours truly — was enough for them.

I put out my paw and batted the silver ball. I looked up at *my* family, and everyone laughed.

Pumpkin's Gift

By PATRICIA CHAPIN

*T*he phone booth stood on the corner of Jen's street and Beacon Street. There was a charming brick, one-story apartment complex on the corner beside it. A wine and cheese store sat directly across the street.

Just as Jen reached the phone, she heard a harsh peal of thunder like the growl of an angry old man. Lightning scratched the sky. Shivering, Jen picked up the receiver. She dialed her old number. She wanted to tell her parents that she was coming home, that she was leaving Robert.

The phone rang for the longest time until, finally, she heard her mother's voice.

"Momma, I can't take it," Jen said, thunder booming overhead. Although she was glad that she'd made up her mind, tears coursed down her cheeks.

"What's the matter, honey?" asked the familiar voice at the other end of the line.

"I said I can't..."

Just then, in the silence between thunder cracks, Jen heard a tiny bleating. Looking down at her feet, she saw a lump of orange fur. He looked up at her and mewed. Then the little kitten coiled around her ankles.

Poor thing, Jen thought, he's going to get soaked in this rain. A few droplets had already begun to fall.

"I'll call you back, Mom," she said.

She replaced the receiver in its cradle, bent down to pick up the tiny ball of fluff and looked into his big green eyes. The eyes, she noticed, were the same color as Robert's.

She was reminded of the way Robert's eyes looked the first time he had asked her out – so big and sweet, like a little boy asking for something special for Christmas. But *he* was the something special. She remembered how he had taken her to a quiet park after dinner and pointed out the constellations to her – Orion, the Pleiades, the Big and Little Dippers. He had said he liked to go to quiet places, to sit perfectly still and see if he could hear the magic of the place. How had Jen forgotten all that?

Now the rain was falling in nickel-sized drops.

"Where's your home, kitty?" she asked.

The kitten had started to purr and he nestled his soft face against her neck. Jen peered through the glass of the phone booth. She saw that one of the apartments had an open door. Holding the purring kitten, she dashed from the shelter of the booth and knocked on the screen.

A young woman came to the door. They looked at each other for a moment through the screen.

"Hi, is this your kitten?" Jen asked.

"That's one of them," the woman said, opening the screen door. "Come on in and meet his brothers and sisters."

Jen stepped into the apartment. It was a studio, barely furnished. She didn't even see a TV. What she did see, however, were professional quality drawings tacked all over the walls and a big piece of half-molded clay in the corner. It looked like the beginning of a statue of a tiger.

"I'm an artist," the woman said, following her gaze.

"Boy, you sure are," Jen observed. The woman smiled at the compliment and scratched the kitten behind the ears.

"You want him?" she asked.

Jen looked down at the kitten. "Well, I'm not planning on staying here."

"Too bad. He sure seems to like you. Have a seat and wait out the rain. My name's Laura." She pushed some kittens off an overstuffed arm chair. Jen sat down, and another kitten crawled into her lap. Laura went to the stove and picked up a kettle.

"You like tea?" she asked. "I got all kinds. Raspberry, Earl Grey, peppermint, you name it."

Jen hadn't spoken to anyone but Robert and their landlord since they'd moved to town three weeks earlier. Now she stared at Laura, amazed at her friendliness. Laura was skinny and had black hair that needed combing. Although Jen knew her mother wouldn't have approved at all, somehow Laura made her feel at home. Something about the way she stood there with one hand on her hip, seeming so direct but at the same time so nice, reminded Jen of her sister, Suzanne.

Another kitten pawed at Jen's foot.

"I'd love some tea. I'll have whatever you're having."

They each settled down with a cup of steaming tea while outside the rain poured down. Inside, the kittens rolled over each other and chased one another madly in circles. All, that is, except the little orange kitten, who perched on Jen's shoulder and whispered in her ear.

"You're not from around here, are you?" Laura asked.

"No," Jen answered. "I guess that's pretty obvious."

Laura laughed. "That's a heavy Southern accent you've got."

Once she started talking about her life, Jen found she couldn't stop. It wasn't long before she revealed that she was planning on leaving Robert so that he could find someone else, someone who could give him the child he so badly wanted.

While Jen talked, Laura sat quietly stroking a kitten. Her blue eyes reminded Laura of the lakes back home. Before Jen knew it, the sun was shining in the western sky and the orange kitten had fallen asleep on her lap. Robert would be home soon.

"Maybe I'll just go ahead and take him with me," she said, petting the kitten's head. Laura nodded.

"Come back and visit. Bring him, too," she said.

Jen smiled to herself. Had Laura forgotten she'd just said she was leaving town? Or had she realized, as Jen herself had, that she was going to stick it out a while longer?

*S*he walked into her own house. For the first time, it didn't seem lonely. The kitten had cried on the way over, but as soon as she put him down, he began to explore the unfamiliar territory. Jen looked around. There were still boxes she hadn't unpacked.

As she opened one of the boxes and took out a few kitchen utensils, Jen remembered how cold she had been to Robert that morning. She'd been sitting on their antique, scroll-arm couch, staring out the window.

"Honey, things will get better. I promise," he had said, leaning down to kiss her on the forehead. She had nodded dully.

"I've got to go now," he said. "If you need me, call the office and they'll give me a message."

"How am I supposed to call the office?" Jen asked. "The phone company still hasn't gotten our phone turned on."

Robert stuck his hand in the pocket of his suit and pulled out some quarters.

"You can use the pay phone down at the end of the street," he said. He put the quarters on the table and kissed her again. Then he walked out, gently closing the door behind him.

As soon as the door closed, Jen began to cry. She didn't like to cry in front of him. She knew the miscarriage, her second, had hurt him, too. But this time was so much worse, far away from family and friends. They had just moved to Boston from Tennessee, and she felt so terribly alone. It was worse than she'd ever imagined.

On their second day in Boston, Jen woke up with wrenching cramps just below her stomach. Everything turned dark; she felt as if a tornado had swept in from nowhere and sucked up all the life inside her.

"No!" she had cried out. "No, no!" Then all she remembered was Robert holding her, saying, "It's all right, honey, it's all right." But it wasn't all right. She had lost another baby.

Jen moved on to the next box. Inside, she found tiny gowns that tied at the bottom like sacks that her family had given her before she'd left home.

She felt the old catch at the heart...

Just then, the kitten leapt like some sort of kamikaze pilot into the pile of clothes. He rolled over, desperately wrestling with the strings of a tiny bonnet. She laughed. It was the first time she had laughed in three weeks. She picked up the kitten and kissed his nose.

"You really are some kind of little miracle," she said. "Before you came along, I never could have looked in this box."

Wiping the perspiration from her neck, Jen shoved the box into a closet. Maybe someday her sister, Suzanne, would need it.

The air was damp and raw. Back home it would be breezy, and the mountains would sweeten the air in the valleys.

She missed home. Every day since coming to Boston, Jen had just sat in the living room of the small, rented house and watched the soap operas churn away on the television. Back home she had been too busy to watch soap operas – except for her favorite one in the late afternoon. She'd had a job teaching every morning at the church preschool.

Now she smiled at the thought of the little children coming to her for their daily hugs and kisses. She remembered the solid feel of their little bodies, ripe and warm, as she'd put them in the swings outside in the play yard and then push them up, up, up, while they squealed with delight.

Jen rubbed her hands over her stomach. After the second miscarriage, she had decided that she'd never try again. The pain was too much to bear. She had fallen in love with this last child. She didn't know if she could ever love again. Even the way she felt about Robert had changed.

When Robert came in the front door that evening, he whistled in admiration.

"Wow, you really got some work done, didn't you?" he said. The boxes had been unpacked. Jen had found some curtains for the window, and she'd rearranged the furniture so that there seemed to be more room.

He sat down and then suddenly jumped up again.

"Ow!" He grabbed his ankle, and a ball of orange fur shot across the living room.

> *A kitten? When did you get a kitten? WHY did you get a kitten?*

"What was that?"

Jen laughed and wrapped her arms around her husband. He was as handsome as ever, his dark hair thick and curly, his green eyes warm. People had said he should be on TV because of his looks. But he was much more than a pretty face, and she knew she was too selfish to let go of him just yet.

"That was a kitten," she answered.

"A kitten? When did you get a kitten? *WHY* did you get a kitten?"

Jen scooped up the animal and kissed his nose. He swatted a

strand of hair that dangled in front of her face.

"I just needed a little company," she said. She felt the old pain choking in her throat, and her eyes welled up with tears.

"Don't cry, Jen," Robert said quickly. "It's just that I'm not that crazy about cats."

As Jen wiped her eyes, she heard him sigh. She knew he was tired of the tears. Every time he'd tried to hold her, to kiss her, to love her, every time he'd touched her since the miscarriage, it seemed to open the floodgates.

"What's for dinner?" he asked.

She pointed to the kitchen. He went in, and she followed, still holding the kitten. He looked down at the dinette table, whirled around and stared at her, an expression of puzzlement on his handsome features.

"Wine and cheese?" he asked.

Jen nodded. "I just got so busy cleaning that I didn't have time to cook something. Remember we had wine and cheese on our honeymoon?"

He smiled and put an arm around her. The kitten crawled up on his shoulder.

"Hey, get off me!" he said. But the kitten just purred.

They took the wine and cheese into the living room. Jen brought out some crackers, and they ate on the floor. The kitten scampered around, and even Robert laughed at his antics.

"What's its name?" Robert asked.

"He doesn't have one yet, do you, pumpkin?" she asked, as if he were one of the kids back at the preschool.

"Pumpkin's a good name," Robert said. "He's orange and all."

Jen's eyes lit up. Pumpkin was the perfect name. Later, after their makeshift picnic, Robert edged closer to her and brought his lips to hers. His kiss was as sweet as honey. Guiltily, she thought of how earlier that day she had planned to leave him. And she wondered if she still should, for his sake.

Then his kiss grew warmer, and although it was dark outside, it was light and cheerful in the house, and she decided that she wouldn't decide anything just then. He lifted her and carried her into the bedroom. Pumpkin had fallen fast asleep in a corner of the couch.

The next day, Jen decided to make sure she wouldn't get pregnant again. She was not going to have any more miscarriages. Pumpkin would be her baby from now on.

*T*he next few weeks passed quickly. She was visiting Laura almost daily and thinking of getting some kind of work. Robert wasn't making much money, and she was getting bored with nothing to do. She also noticed she was putting on a little weight.

"I need to get some money so I can start working out again," Jen told Laura one day while watching her paint a picture of the Charles River. "My sister and I used to go to aerobics classes every day back home."

"You must be pretty good," Laura said, dabbing some blue watercolor into the green. They were sitting on a park bench, overlooking the wide, calm river. Pumpkin lay curled on Jen's lap. The sound of his purring relaxed Jen. It was mid-April and one of those rare days when the sun's warmth poured over them like warm honey.

"I was pretty good. I liked it," Jen answered.

"Then why don't you become an instructor? That would solve both of your problems. I saw a sign down at that aerobics center by the supermarket," Laura said.

Jen's jaw dropped. "I never thought of that! One thing I know is that I don't want to work with children. I don't think I could ever do that again." Laura looked at her and smiled, her eyes warm with sympathy.

To Jen's delight, she was hired to teach two classes, three days a week. But Robert didn't seem as happy as she did.

"When are we going to try to have a baby again, Jen?" he asked. Pumpkin lay between them on the big, king-sized bed. He stroked the cat's soft fur.

"I thought you understood, Robert. I can't do that again. You're a man, so you don't know what I went through," she said with a scowl.

"That's not fair," he replied. "You don't know what I went through, either. I just don't see why you have to give up."

He got out of bed and headed for the living room. She heard the TV come on. Sometimes she couldn't stand him. But maybe he was right, she thought. Maybe I'm a coward, she said to herself. She should leave him and let him find someone who could have a baby for him.

Pumpkin grabbed her fingers between his claws, and she pulled him toward her.

"What am I going to do, Pumpkin?" she asked. The kitten blinked at her. She scratched his ears and soon fell asleep with her arms around him.

The ladies at the aerobics center loved her.

"You have the cutest Southern accent," they told her. "And the nicest smile."

One day, when she'd been working at the center about a month, Jen was leading her class as usual. They had just done their warm-ups and started into the first fast aerobics song when she felt herself begin to tire. She figured she hadn't gotten enough sleep. She and Robert had been fighting again – this time over nothing. It didn't seem to take much to get them started anymore.

By the end of the set, she realized she was really exhausted. She could barely keep up with the women who were supposed to be following her.

When she got home, she fell right to sleep. The next morning, she rushed to the bathroom and vomited. Robert was still asleep. I can't do this again, Jen said to herself. I just can't go through it.

She leaned against the kitchen wall and gazed around her at the clock on the wall, the Currier & Ives plates on the shelves, the mugs hanging from hooks by the sink. It was a small kitchen with large green tiles on the floor. She had the strange sensation that she had never seen it before.

Then she felt something warm and soft moving against her ankles. She lifted Pumpkin and listened to the soft sound of his purring. He nuzzled one of her ear lobes. It was then that Jen knew that she would give her body another chance.

"We won't tell Robert yet," she whispered to Pumpkin. "I don't want to get his hopes up again." The cat just closed his eyes as if to say he wouldn't tell a soul.

Jen switched to a light aerobics class once a day. Her doctor had asked her to consider not teaching any classes at all. But somehow she knew that if the pregnancy was going to work, nothing could stop it, and if not, well, then nothing would make it work.

*M*ay rolled into June, and June slid into July. Although she and Robert didn't fight, there was a distance between them, as if they were standing on opposite sides of a lake, watching each other across the distance, but unable to talk. Even though she knew it would help, she couldn't bring herself to tell him yet.

Both she and Pumpkin grew larger and rounder as the weeks went by. Then one late Sunday afternoon in August, Jen was sitting on the couch, cradling the cat like a baby. Robert came into the room and stared at her. She could feel the warmth of the sunlight shining through the windows, and she could smell the sweet scent of the rose bushes growing outside.

"Why didn't you tell me?" he asked. She looked up at him. He crossed the room and knelt on the floor in front of her. "Jen! I can see it all over your face!"

31

"I was afraid you'd be disappointed again," she said, her eyes filling with tears. Robert kissed each tear away. Pumpkin lay between them, purring loudly.

The baby was due on the twelfth of January. On Christmas Eve, Laura brought over a watercolor she'd done of a clown walking a chicken on a leash.

"It's for the baby's room," she told them. Jen hugged her and kissed her cheek.

"Boy, you sure are big," Laura said. "Are you sure that baby isn't due for another three weeks?"

"We're sure," Robert said, draping a protective arm over Jen. Jen smiled and rubbed her belly. She had always wanted this feeling, and now here it was, tight and powerful. She felt as if she alone were keeping the world turning in its orb.

Laura bent down to give Pumpkin's head a scratch. "Look at the way he smiles," she said. "Like he's got a secret."

> ❛*Look at the way he smiles... like he's got a secret.*❜

"He always looks like that," Jen replied. "I think he knew all along that I was going to have a baby this time." Pumpkin looked up at her with his big green marble eyes and blinked.

"Are you sure you don't want to come to church with us, Laura?" Robert asked. He was already dressed in his suit and tie. The Christmas tree twinkled in the corner of the room. Jen and Robert had already discovered that they'd better put the breakable ornaments on top. Pumpkin was teaching them a thing or two about baby-proofing.

"No thanks, Robert," Laura said with a smile. "I'll pass this time"

"Well, all right," he said. "Just wanted to let you know you were welcome to join us."

"Thanks," she said, and kissed him on the cheek. She patted Jen's belly and left.

On the way to the church, Robert took Jen's hand.

"Why so quiet, honey?" he asked.

Jen sighed. "I know I should be happy," she said, "but it's freezing and it doesn't feel like Christmas without my family here. Back home, Mom will be worrying about every little thing. Daddy will be making his usual bad jokes, and Suzanne will have some crazy idea that everyone should go on a scavenger hunt or something. Then the whole family is going to be having a big turkey dinner with cranberries and potatoes and sweet potato pie. And we'll be here, eating hot dogs and corn chips."

"We could make a turkey," Robert said, as he pulled the car into the church parking lot.

"It's not the turkey, Robert," she said, struggling out of the car. He came around the car and took her hand and she tried to smile at him as they walked inside.

The service was nice, and the Christmas carols made Jen feel a little better. If only she could have been with the rest of her family! The people here were all friendly enough, but it wasn't the same. It wasn't like the people she had known all her life. It felt funny to have her baby in a town where she hardly knew anybody at all. She wondered what it would be like for her child to grow up here, so different from the wooded hills where she'd grown up.

After the service, they walked out into the night air and climbed back into their car. Robert turned the ignition. Then the pains began. "It's time honey..." she said through gritted teeth.

His face went pale, and his eyes grew wide and bright.

"Which way is the hospital?" he asked, his eyes wide and his voice quivering. "Don't have the baby yet, Jen! Hold on, now."

"I'm not going to have the baby yet. Just go to the house and get the bag and then we'll go to the hospital," she said. The day before, they had packed the bag with her spare gown, her fuzzy socks, her toiletries, the paper bag for breathing, the candy to suck on and all the other things they had learned they would need.

Through everything, Jen felt a strange calm. It was three weeks early, but after everything she had been through, she knew she could bring her baby safely into the world.

Robert, on the other hand, was beside himself.

"Are you all right? Do you think the baby's all right? Jen, stay calm," he said, his voice cracking.

"I'm fine, Robert. And I think the baby will be fine," she murmured.

At the hospital, an orderly wheeled her into her room. Her doctor was called, and he began preparing her for the birth.

When the pains became more regular, they were terrible. Jen stared at a picture of a house on the wall and tried to imagine that her family was there. She would imagine there was a big table inside laden with silver and china and Christmas dinner. Then a pain would strike, and the image would disappear.

Every time she looked up, she saw Robert's handsome face, filled with worry and yet so full of love and admiration for her that she clenched in the pain and let it wash over her.

At six o'clock, Jen went into the final transition, and, twenty minutes later, their baby girl took her first breath. She looked over and saw the doctor hand the tiny, naked life into Robert's arms. Robert brought the baby to her, and she saw tears spilling down Robert's cheeks.

"Merry Christmas," he said, placing the newborn into Jen's arms. Jen was soon wheeled into another room. She and the baby, whom they'd named Christa, fell asleep curled around each other like two kittens.

Later that night, Robert brought a framed picture of Pumpkin and set it on the table beside Jen's bed. They sat together watching Christa, who was sleeping in a bassinet by the bed.

"This is a Christmas I'll never forget," Jen said. Looking out the window, she could see Christmas lights twinkling all over as if the city were one big jewel sparkling on a velvet glove.

"Jen, I've been thinking," Robert said. "Maybe we should move back home. I could get my old job back." As he spoke, he twirled the wedding band around his finger.

Jen reached over and took his hand.

"Come close to me," she said. He held her tighter. She could feel his warmth wrapping around her. She thought of how she loved the way his eyes roved over her face whenever he was close to her, as if he were caressing her with feathers.

Jen nestled against her husband's shoulder and stroked his long, powerful fingers. The gold wedding band gleamed in the moonlight.

"Home is wherever my family is," she said. "This family, I mean. You, Christa, me, and, of course, Pumpkin."

The baby made a soft, sleepy noise in her bassinet. And the cat in the picture smiled at them as if to say, "You're welcome."

The Cat Who Went North

By NEIL PLAKCY

I started to worry after we crossed the state border from North Carolina into Virginia.

"I don't know about you, Pilar," I said to my cat, who lay comfortably in her carrier on the front seat next to me, "but I think this is pretty cold."

I tuned the radio until I found one of those all-news AM stations and concentrated on driving north on the interstate until the weather report came on. It was 52 degrees out and heading for the 40's.

"The forties!" I exclaimed. It was only November. In Key West, which I'd just left, it almost never got that cold. Well, maybe a day or two in January, but then the cold front would blow over and the sun would come out, and I'd be back in my shorts again.

"I'm not really sure about this," I said to Pilar. Since she had adopted me three years before, I had developed the habit of thinking out loud and addressing my thoughts to Pilar, a red, gold and black Abyssinian with extra toes on each paw.

Pilar is a Hemingway cat, a descendant of the cats that lived in the Ernest Hemingway house in Key West. The woman who sold Pilar to me had explained that to be a Hemingway, a cat had to have at least one extra toe on one paw. They charged a base price for their cats and then extra for each spare toe.

By the time we'd gotten back to my apartment, I'd decided to name her Pilar, after Hemingway's boat and after the heroine of *For Whom the Bell Tolls*. She seemed to accept the name.

"What do you think, Pilar?" I asked. "Should we turn around and head back to Key West? After all, this is only a job. Do I really want to work and live in Philadelphia?"

Pilar mewed.

"Well, yes, you're right, it is a good job," I said. After years of struggle, working at every hotel position from bellhop to dining room waiter to front desk clerk, I had settled in as the marketing director for a property that was part of a national chain.

I'd done a good job and been offered a promotion, as director of marketing for a much larger hotel in the chain in Philadelphia. I was going to be making real money for the first time in my life, and I had thought that it would be exciting to leave Key West, where I was born and raised, to live in a big, fascinating city like Philadelphia.

But as I drove farther north, and the weather got colder, I was starting to have doubts.

"There's an exit up ahead," I said to Pilar. "I could turn around and start heading south again. We could make it to Georgia by dark."

Pilar was silent.

"You're not being much help," I said. "Tell you what. If you don't say anything, I'll keep going. If you think I should turn around, then say something."

I turned to look at my cat, curled up in a corner of her carrier. She yawned and rolled onto her side.

"What was that?" I asked. "Was that a yes or a no?"

Pilar went to sleep. "I guess I keep going," I said.

*M*y furniture was waiting for us when we arrived in Philadelphia, in an apartment not far from the hotel. The chain had been great, finding me this place and arranging everything for me.

As soon as I let Pilar into the apartment, she prowled every corner, sniffing and investigating everything in her new surroundings. Cats are naturally very curious, and Abyssinians, who are among the most intelligent of all cats, are also among the nosiest. Pilar is a prime example.

She loves to poke around in my things. She has a habit of getting into half-open drawers, nudging open cupboard doors with her nose, even digging the dirt out of my potted plants. Before I leave for anything more than just a day at work, I do what I call 'cat-proofing'. Cat-proofing the apartment means making it as secure as I can, keeping as much as possible away from Pilar's prying paws.

On the morning of my first day at work, I decided to take no chances and cat-proofed the apartment as best I could. I bundled up in a T-shirt, a blue oxford-cloth button down shirt over that, a sweater and a cream-colored linen sports jacket, and set out for work.

The first thing I learned about living in a cold climate was that I had all the wrong clothes. In Key West, I wore a tie to work, and long pants, but most of the time I lived in shorts, T-shirts, and deck shoes without socks. Everything in my closet was cotton or linen, and I didn't even own an overcoat.

But things were different in Philadelphia. Even with all my layers, I was still cold that first day. I was sitting in my new office, rubbing my hands together, when Lisa Audubon, director of food and beverage, stuck her head in the door.

We had met earlier that morning, when the general manager had taken me around and introduced me to the staff. She was a very pretty green-eyed blonde, with a Southern accent that knocked my socks off. Down in Key West, we may be south of the Mason-Dixon line, but we're south of everything else, too. Most of the Floridians I grew up with talked more like they were from New York than from New Orleans.

"Bet you're cold," Lisa said.

"How'd you know?"

"I moved here last year from Atlanta," she said. "Took me weeks to feel warm again."

"Don't tell me that! This is just my first day."

"I can help," Lisa said. "After work, I'm going to take you to a great store. As long as you've got a credit card that you haven't charged to the limit, they can put you into some warm clothes."

"That would be terrific." I also thought it would be terrific to get a chance to check out that golden hair, those green eyes, and that sweet-as-sugar accent.

"I'm finished at six," she said. "How about you?"

"Six is good." I thought of Pilar. "But I have to check in on my cat. I need to make sure she's adjusting."

"I don't like cats," Lisa said. "I tell you what. The store's not too far from here. If I give you the address, can you meet me there at, say, six-thirty?"

So at six o'clock, I bundled myself up as well as I could and drove home to check on Pilar. I found her curled up on the bed, most of her body hidden away under a pillow. I turned up the thermostat a few degrees.

"I'm going out again," I called to her from the kitchen, where I put out some dinner in her bowl and changed her water. "I'm coming back with lots of warm clothes."

Pilar said nothing.

Lisa was great. She helped me pick out wool pants, a lined overcoat and gloves, then held up a green, loden-cloth blazer with brown leather buttons.

"This jacket is a good color for you," she said. "The leather matches your hair, and the green makes your eyes look a lot darker, don't you think?"

I looked in the mirror. My eyes were hazel, a watery greenish brown that I'd never found very flattering. But sure enough, when I wore that jacket, they looked darker.

We walked around the store, pillaging department after department. I got a scarf, a couple of sweaters, another wool blazer and some long-sleeved shirts. By the time I was done, my credit card was warm to the touch.

"Can I buy you dinner?" I asked. "To say thanks for the help?"

"Sure." I loved the way her smooth voice caressed that single word. I had to come to Philadelphia to find a Southern girl, I thought.

By the time we'd had dinner, and I got home, it was already late. Pilar rocketed around the living room a few times, and when she finally stopped and came up to me, she mewed, accusing me of abandonment. She walked around me once, sniffed and then shot down the hall.

"What's the matter?" I asked. I followed her into the bedroom, where I finally managed to coax her onto my lap.

"That's just Lisa. Somebody at work who was nice to me today. You're going to have to get used to me coming home with all different smells on me."

I got undressed, pulled down the covers on the bed and got in. Pilar snuggled up next to my stomach. In a few minutes, she was purring.

I settled into my job pretty easily. It was, after all, the same thing I'd done in Key West, only at a larger hotel.

When a cold front swept into Philadelphia, I caught the sniffles, but a combination of hot toddies and over-the-counter remedies carried me through.

Lisa was sympathetic. I didn't see her much during the day, but occasionally our paths would cross and she'd give me pointers on life in a cold climate. On Saturday night, we went to dinner and the movies.

"I'm always cold," I confessed over dinner. "I guess my blood is thin, from living in Florida." I leaned back against the banquette. "Pilar doesn't like the cold weather here, either. She's not happy. I can tell."

Lisa shook her head. "She's inside all day where it's warm. How can she know the difference?"

"She knows," I said. "When I come home, she's racing around the apartment, like she's trying to get warm. Her fur's thicker, and she's been very frisky lately, always wanting to play. She hasn't been this playful since she was a little kitten."

"It sounds to me like she likes it here. 'Frisky, playful'. Those aren't adjectives you use to describe an unhappy cat."

I wasn't sure how to answer that. MY life was certainly different, but I had to admit Pilar was still in familiar surroundings, warm and comfortable every day. I had discovered when I got my first electric bill that I paid for heat, and it was very expensive, so I kept the thermometer at 68 while I was at work. It wasn't what Pilar was accustomed to, but it wasn't cold, either.

"You have to know her like I do," I finally said. "For example, she's not a very affectionate cat. She's not the type to come and curl up on your lap all the time. But here, as soon as I sit down, she comes to snuggle up against me."

The waiter brought the check. We paid and stood up to put our coats on. That was something I had a hard time getting accustomed to, all that time spent dressing and undressing before going out. In Key West, all you had to do was throw on a sweater if it was cool.

"Why don't you come up to my place for a nightcap?" I asked. "It's just around the corner."

She pursed her lips. "Won't Pilar mind?"

"We're going to have to find that out sooner or later."

When we got to my apartment, though, Pilar put on her company behavior. That is, she hid under the bed and wouldn't come out.

"That's fine with me," Lisa said. "I told you I'm not really a cat person."

My apartment had a fireplace, something I'd had no experience with in Key West. The previous tenant had left some logs in the grate, and Lisa helped me make a fire. She and I sat on the sofa together in companionable silence.

"This is nice," I said. "I see why people like fireplaces."

"It's one of the ways people keep warm here," Lisa said.

"That and warm clothes." I grinned and tapped my pants leg. "The wonder of wool."

"There are other ways people keep warm up here," she said. "I can show you, if you're interested." She snuggled up close to me and laid her lovely blonde head on my shoulder.

"I'm interested," I said. I put my arm around her, and she lifted her face up to mine. It shone golden in the firelight. We kissed. "I'm interested all right," I said.

We kissed again. Suddenly I felt a huge, furry weight on my neck.

"Pilar," I said. I drew back from Lisa and pulled my cat onto my lap. "This is Lisa, Pilar," I said. "Lisa, meet Pilar."

Lisa was pulling cat hairs from her face. "I guessed."

"Let me put her away." I stood up and carried Pilar down the hall, where I locked her in the bedroom.

"Sorry, Pilar," I said, tossing her gently onto the bed,

where she landed gracefully on all fours. "Be good now."

I returned to Lisa on the couch. Within minutes, Pilar started to howl, a scratchy, high-pitched noise that raised hairs on the back of my neck.

"She's never acted like this before," I said. "Let's try and ignore her."

We kissed again, but it was hard to concentrate, what with Pilar caterwauling in the background.

"I think she's jealous," Lisa said.

"Probably." I stood up. "I'm sorry, I just can't listen to that." I went to the bedroom and opened the door. Pilar had pulled a pair of my new wool pants off the door and onto the floor and curled them into a nest. I could see a place where her claw had caught in the fabric.

"Pilar!" I tried to grab her, but she darted between my legs and out to the living room.

When I followed her out, Lisa was standing by the door, holding her coat.

"I'd better go," she said. "I'll see you at work on Monday."

"See what you did?" I said to Pilar when Lisa had gone. "You ruined my evening, and you ruined my new pants!"

But Pilar wouldn't hang around to listen to my complaints. She settled down beside the dying fire and dozed off contentedly, her evening's work done.

I wasn't about to give up on Lisa so easily. Even with my new clothes, I was still cold all the time, and she was the only warm thing in my life, besides Pilar.

43

I spent most of every day in my office, on the phone and at the computer, making and renewing contacts with the press and writing releases. One of our big events in mid-December was an ice-sculpture contest, held in one of our ballrooms that opened to the outdoors. I had to work long hours in the days before the event and planned to stay overnight at the hotel the weekend the exhibit was open.

On the first day of the exhibit, I was so rushed that I hurried out of the apartment, just barely making sure that Pilar had enough food and water to last her until Sunday.

The sculptures were placed on tables all around the room, with several large pieces on pedestals in the center. Coming from Key West, I hadn't had much experience with ice sculpture, and I was surprised at the variety. There were penguins and polar bears, and an igloo with an Eskimo next to it, dressed in a fur parka that was so realistic you could almost feel the softness of the fur.

*W*e had the doors wide open, and the larger sculptures were placed in the circular drive outside. I was rushing inside and out nearly all weekend, suffering through the frigid air as I walked reporters around and introduced them to the people who had done the carvings. Then I had to stand there, my hands in my pockets and my face turning blue, while the reporters asked questions and took note of the answers.

By Sunday afternoon, I had a real cold going. I kept shivering, and my nose wouldn't stop running. At six o'clock the exhibit closed down, and as soon as the last guest walked out the door I headed home for some aspirin and hot tea, and a snuggle under my new goosedown quilt.

As soon as I walked in the door, I could see something was wrong.

My clothes lay scattered around the living room. Pilar had scooped dirt out of my potted hibiscus (which was slowly dying anyway) and stepped in it. She had marched all over

44

my clean shirts and pants, even my underwear.

In the kitchen, she'd opened the cupboard and spilled oatmeal and pasta all over the counters. She'd shredded a roll of paper towels and knocked over the caddy with my spatulas and other kitchen tools in it. I had grown up around photos of the disastrous Key West hurricane of 1926, and my apartment looked just like those pictures.

I stood in the doorway surveying the horror in front of me. Pilar came dashing out of the bedroom, and she didn't seem to understand or care that I was sick. She wanted to play. She batted her ball to me, but I knocked it away. I went into the kitchen, drank orange juice right out of the carton and then went into the bedroom.

> ‘ *She batted her ball to me, but I knocked it away.* ’

The scene there was just as bad as in the living room. A long trail of toilet paper stretched toward the bathroom, and the books and papers that had been on my bureau were on the floor. My clothing was everywhere. I took off what I was wearing and dropped it on the pile, then crawled into bed.

Pilar jumped up and tried to snuggle next to me.

"Bad cat," I murmured, pushing her away. It did no good. She curled up next to me, and we both fell asleep.

By morning, I felt even worse. When I called in sick, my secretary told me, "And don't come in until you get better. You'll infect the whole hotel."

"Thanks," I said. For a while I wrapped myself in the quilt and watched TV in the living room, barely bothering to clear a space for myself on the couch. Then I went back to bed.

The door buzzer woke me around six-thirty. I stumbled to the intercom.

"Who is it?"

"It's Lisa. I brought you a get-well package."

I surveyed the room. It looked terrible. Then I shrugged and said, "That's really nice. Come on up."

Lisa looked beautiful. Her shimmering hair was piled up in a loose bun, and her cheeks were ruddy from the cold.

She took one look around and said, "What happened? Did you get robbed?"

"A cat burglar," I replied. I looked around for Pilar, but she was hiding again. "The culprit is lying low at the moment."

"You look terrible," Lisa said. "Go on back to bed. I'll take care of things for you."

I started to protest, feebly, but she pushed me toward the bedroom, saying, "I'll call you when the soup is ready."

When I got into bed, Pilar appeared out of the shadows and jumped up next to me.

"You really know how to make me look bad," I said to her.

I started to pet her. Abyssinians have very soft fur, almost like rabbit. Each hair has about five different bands of color on it, shades of red and black and cream. Her fur felt smooth.

Then Lisa called, "Soup's on," from the kitchen, and Pilar shot away from me, toward the closet.

The soup was delicious. Lisa had also brought more aspirin, a heating pad, a hot water bottle and three different kinds of cold medicine.

"This is so nice of you," I said. "I could just kiss you."

"Save it for when you're better," she said. "That looks like a rotten cold, and I don't want to catch it." She stood up and started clearing the table. "Now you go back to bed, and I'll clean up in here."

"You don't have to," I protested. "I can do it in the morning."

"Don't be ridiculous. Now scoot."

I went back into the bedroom and got into bed.

"Pilar," I called. "Here, girl."

She didn't answer. I wondered where she was. I heard Lisa

start running water in the kitchen sink, and suddenly I knew. I jumped out of bed, but before I'd even made it to the bedroom door I heard Lisa.

"Oh, no!" she shrieked. "You...cat!"

Unlike most cats, Abyssinians love water. In Key West, where I had had a tub shower with a curtain, Pilar often loved to come into the shower with me and play under the spray. Whenever I did the dishes, I had to shove her away from the countertop because she liked to play in the sudsy water.

When I reached the kitchen I found Lisa trying to dry herself off with a hand towel.

"Your cat jumped in the sink," she said. "She splashed water all over me." There was a big place on her peacock blue blouse where the fabric had gone dark, and another big dark spot on her ivory-colored skirt.

"I'm sorry."

"This is a silk blouse." She wouldn't meet my gaze.

"I'll pay for the cleaning," I said. "I'm sorry. She's not usually like this. She's just mad that I was at the hotel all weekend."

"Well, I wasn't too crazy that you had to work either, but at least I'm doing something constructive!"

I didn't really have an answer to that.

"Go back to sleep," she said finally. "But take your cat with you, please."

I knelt down on the floor. "Come here, Pilar," I said.

But she wouldn't come. She crouched under the sofa and stared. I was just too sick to get down and drag her out.

> *Your cat jumped in the sink... she splashed water all over me.*

Instead, I stood up, walked over to the corner of the room and picked up her red rubber ball. A few weeks after I bought Pilar, I discovered that she loved to fetch. It was an odd kind of revelation; fetching was something I'd always associated with dogs rather than with cats. But after reading up on her breed, I'd found that they do like to play ball.

Now I tossed her ball back and forth from hand to hand for a moment or two. Lisa stood with her arms crossed, and Pilar watched intently from her place under the sofa. I backed toward the hallway, tossing the ball back and forth, back and forth. When I finally reached the hall, I stopped. I turned my back to Pilar and then quickly threw her ball out into the living room.

Just as I expected, she shot out from under the sofa and raced into the living room. She jumped up and caught the ball in her paws on one of its bounces. Then she turned around and brought it right back to me in her mouth.

"Gotcha," I said, feeling a little guilty as I grabbed hold of her. I looked over my shoulder at Lisa as we left the room. "We'll be in the bedroom."

Pilar mewed in my arms. She struggled to get away, but I wouldn't let go. I closed the door behind us and got back into bed. She sat by the door and mewed loudly, but I ignored her. Within a very few minutes I was asleep.

> *She sat by the door and mewed loudly, but I ignored her.*

I didn't hear Lisa leave, but sometime in the night I woke up to go to the bathroom. When I went back to bed, I left the bedroom door open.

When I woke the next morning, I sat up in bed. My body still ached, but my nose had stopped running, and I could breathe a little easier.

The bedroom was still a mess, but I actually felt like I might do some cleaning. Then I looked at the open door.

"Oh, no," I said. I got out of bed and walked out to the living room to see what further damage Pilar had done.

To my amazement, the room was spotless, and Pilar was sleeping quietly in a patch of sun near the front window.

"It's a miracle," I said. "If I knew the patron saint of cats, I'd say a blessing."

I fixed a little breakfast and called the office for my messages. Then I cleaned up the bedroom, watched a bit of TV and reheated Lisa's leftover chicken soup for lunch. Around three o'clock, I got dressed.

"I'm not going away for long this time," I told Pilar. "So don't go crazy on me, OK?"

Pilar sat up from her place on the dining room table and stretched. I put down my briefcase and picked up her ball.

"Come on," I said. "Want to play catch?" I tossed the ball in her direction.

She must have thought I was going to lock her up again, because she didn't move. I walked over to the ball and picked it up, then tossed it again, right at her. This time she couldn't help herself. She jumped up in the air and caught it with her front paws. When she landed back on the table, she skidded a little, but stopped herself by scratching her claws into the finish.

Pilar often jumps up to catch balls that are tossed to her, grabbing them with her extra toes, which she uses almost like thumbs. I've even seen her use them to pick up her dry food and dip it into her water. We played catch for a little while, just until I felt that she'd forgiven me for locking her up the night before. Then I drove over to the hotel.

I didn't want to do too much. I looked over the mail and the phone messages and returned a few calls. By five o'clock, I was ready to leave, but I stopped by Lisa's office first.

"She's in the Franklin Ballroom," her secretary said. "Big dinner tonight."

The Franklin was one of our smaller ballrooms, on the second floor of the hotel. It was nice for intimate dinner parties of say, fifty or so. That day, it had been set up with round tables and a lectern at the back of the room, obviously for some kind of corporate or awards dinner. Though the cloths were on the tables, they hadn't been set yet, and the folding chairs were still stacked at the side of the room.

Lisa was rearranging the flowers in the centerpiece on the table closest to the door. When she saw me, she sighed.

"What's the matter?" I asked.

"The client asked for carnations," she said, "and said no roses." There was a pile of red carnations on her left, and a pile of red roses pulled out of the centerpiece on her right.

"Can I help?"

"Sure. Grab some carnations."

*W*hile we worked, the set-up staff began putting out the chairs, and the waiters laid out the place settings and folded the napkins. I felt comfortable working with Lisa, and I decided I was finally settling into my job and the new hotel. The new city was going to take a little longer to get used to, for me and Pilar, but I thought we were well on our way.

We finished the flowers as the first of the guests arrived.

"Thanks," she said, as we walked down the hall toward the food and beverage office.

"I'm the one who owes you some thanks," I said. "Big time. You didn't have to clean my apartment for me."

"You didn't look like you were in any shape to do it," she said. Then she looked at me in not quite mock horror.

"You didn't let the cat into the living room, did you?"

"She got out in the middle of the night," I said. "And she didn't do a thing. I was really surprised." I smiled. "Come on, get your coat, and let me buy you a drink."

We had reached the door of her office. She stopped there and shook her head.

"You ought to get home. Do you still have some soup left?"

"Absolutely. It was delicious, by the way."

"My mother's recipe. You go home, have some soup and get a good night's sleep. You can buy me that drink later."

Then and there I knew that whatever it took to keep that girl, short of giving away my cat, that is, I would do.

I stopped at the grocery and picked up a few things, including a nice piece of fresh salmon for Pilar, something to give her when I needed a bribe.

When I got home, she was pacing in front of the window. One of the things I've always admired about her is her sleek, regal bearing. They say that Abyssinians were prized cats in the days of the Pharaohs, and you can see pictures of them in Egyptian paintings. Seeing her stalk back and forth like that, I could easily believe Pilar was descended from queens.

"See, I wasn't away too long," I said. "Just like I promised." I went into the kitchen and put down my groceries, and Pilar joined me there, jumping up on the counter.

"You were a naughty cat yesterday," I said. "You shouldn't have splashed Lisa's blouse."

She meowed and began to nose around the grocery bags. Like a true Abyssinian, she had to sniff everything I brought into the house and give it her personal stamp of approval.

I put away the groceries and heated up the last of the chicken soup. Pilar stood on the counter, rubbing against me as I worked.

"What am I going to do about you?" I asked. She meowed and I rubbed her head. I decided I'd give her the salmon.

*B*y the weekend I was feeling better, although I was still getting chills now and then. Lisa and I went to dinner and to the movies, and she came up to my apartment afterward.

"Don't worry," I said as we walked in. "I'll make sure Pilar stays in the bedroom."

Pilar was waiting by the front door, but as soon as she saw Lisa she skittered under the sofa.

"She may warm up to you sometime," I said. "At least she's behaving now."

51

"Maybe she'll even like me one day," Lisa said. I took her coat, and we went over to the sofa. "I'm not a bad person."

"I'd agree with that. You just happen to be a person who doesn't like cats."

We sat down on the sofa and Lisa stretched out. I pulled her shoes off, rested her feet in my lap, and stroked them.

"It's not exactly true that I don't like cats," she said.

"What do you mean? Usually you're either a cat person or not. I haven't met many in-betweens."

"I used to have a Siamese," she began. "For about five years. Her name was Nanki-Poo, from *The Mikado*." She paused. "She was an indoors cat. The only times she ever went out was to the vet, in her carrier. One day when I was bringing in my groceries, I left the door open, and she got out."

"Oh, no," I murmured.

"She chased a bird into the street, and a car hit her."

"I'm really sorry."

"So I don't like to be around cats. They remind me of her."

"If anything happened to Pilar, I'd feel awful," I said.

And then, to my surprise, Pilar crawled out from under the sofa. She sat up next to Lisa's hand and purred.

Lisa reached down to scratch behind her ears, and Pilar mewed and rolled over on her back.

I let out a low whistle. "Talk about mood swings!"

"Whose?" Lisa asked. "Pilar's or mine?" She leaned down to rub Pilar's stomach, and the cat purred contentedly.

"Both," I replied.

Lisa grinned. "Maybe she just needed to hear my story."

"Yeah, right."

Pilar jumped up on the sofa between us, and Lisa and I rubbed her tummy together for a minute or two. Then I stood up.

"Let's build a fire," I said, "so we can all warm up."

As soon as the words were out of my mouth, Pilar jumped up

and raced around the room a few times. She finally landed by the fireplace, where she used her paws and her mouth to drag a piece of newspaper toward the fireplace.

Lisa and I looked at each other and laughed.

"Come on," she said. "It'll go faster if the three of us do it."

She patted Pilar's back, and my fickle cat curled up at her feet and purred contentedly.

I didn't argue. She certainly seemed to know what she was talking about.

A Collar for Chocolate

By KATHERINE MOSHER

*W*hen I was a little girl, I was always asking Santa for a kitten at Christmas. A kitten headed all my Christmas lists and began all my conversations with shopping-mall Santas. I clipped pictures out of magazines, wrote on them, "This is the kind of cat I want," and posted them all around the house – on the bathroom mirror, the refrigerator and my parents' bedroom door.

Come Christmas Eve, while my brother poked and prodded at the presents laid enticingly beneath the tree on Christmas Eve, I helped my mother prepare dinner or decorate the house. I knew that Santa wouldn't bring my present until Christmas day – it was that special. I would sleep deeply and dream of fuzzy, four-legged animals chasing bouncy balls of ribbon across my bed.

But no matter how often I asked, I never got a kitten. When I was ten or eleven, and learned that Santa wasn't going to be any help to me, I asked my parents for a cat. I learned then why our Christmas tree never had a little kitten under it.

"Heather," they told me, "you're allergic to cats. We can't get one. You would be miserable."

That Christmas I got a goldfish, complete with five-gallon aquarium and plants and rocks. It was a small orange fish with scales that looked a little like stripes. I named him Morris.

After nearly fifteen years of allergy treatments and injections, I had outgrown the allergies. I still didn't own a cat, however. The apartment I lived in doesn't allow them. I could have moved to another one, but my fiance, Bill, owned the complex. I would have felt funny leaving for a more flexible housing arrangement.

Neighborhood cats would sometimes sniff around the apartments, begging for food. Whenever I'd see one, I'd leave a bowl of milk out for it. The cats never got close enough for me to pet them, but two came about once every other week. I named the orange tabby with the black collar Miles, and the Siamese with white paws was Inches. I kept a small cache of food in my cupboard for them. Bill knew and disapproved, but he didn't forbid me the small comfort. He just looked at me and shook his head. He never had a cat as a child, either. But then, he didn't want one.

Bill and I met two years ago at a housewarming party. It was right around Halloween, and the weather had already turned cold. The sweater he wore was deep green and matched the color of his eyes. There was a hole in the sleeve. He says that I mentioned it to him when we were introduced, but I don't remember that.

Someone took a picture of us at that party. It's in my scrapbook. My shoulder-length hair was longer then, and Bill had a mustache. He drove me home that night, and I let him kiss me good night. The very next day, he called and asked if I would like to see a play. We saw the closing performance of a silly, slapstick comedy about a man with two wives.

We discovered we shared interests in Steve Martin, Shakespeare and the old sitcom *M*A*S*H*. Or maybe that came later. I've lost track; everything happened so fast after that night. It wasn't long before we were sending Christmas gifts together and planning a March marriage.

*T*his past Christmas, stores were open late, red ribbons and bows decorated the street lamps, and harried parents bustled from mall to mall, searching for the perfect toy. For the first year I could remember, I had finished shopping early. I spent the extra time relaxing and watching TV reruns of *Miracle on 34th Street* and *It's a Wonderful Life* with Bill.

I had to work late the last Monday before Christmas. Nearly everyone had left early, hoping to hit the malls before they closed. Only two others – Brian and Carol – and I were left.

I work in a small advertising firm. It's a steady, nine to five job, and it pays well. I have no particular attachment to the work itself; like most places, the people make the job. And the people there are wonderful.

The office is in a small, one-story renovated house. The walls were knocked out long ago to make room for the partitions and desks. In the back room, which used to be a laundry room, we keep a microwave and a small refrigerator.

On a break, I went to the back room for a cup of coffee to go with the danish that had been sitting on my desk since lunch. The room was unusually cold. Someone had left the back door wide open.

The winter sun had already set, and the sky was black. Few stars were visible – but there was a gorgeous full moon. Sometimes it's difficult living in a suburb of a big city. Rush-hour traffic buzzed by the door. Irate motorists honked and yelled at each other.

Children played underneath the street lights in the park across the street. They were building a snowman. Somehow their laughter and yelling carried across the street above the noise of the traffic. Their bright caps and jackets were stained strange colors under the lights and stood out from the snow, making it seem like their clothes were building the snowman by themselves. I closed the door.

I walked back to my office and rounded the corner to my desk. Sitting daintily on my paperwork, eating the last of my cherry danish, was a small, black-striped kitten. I blinked in surprise. I stayed quiet. I watched her from the door, letting her finish. Her fur was soft and shiny, her paws and face neatly groomed. Her delicate bones protruded slightly from her body. No scratch marks or cuts marred her coat. This was obviously someone's pet. But she didn't have a collar.

When she was through, the cat looked up at me, licking the last of the frosting off her face. I approached cautiously. Two yellow-green eyes watched me intently. I expected her to let me get about four feet away before bolting out the office door.

Four feet, three feet, two feet... This was definitely someone's pet.

The kitten sniffed my fingers and then rubbed her head up against my knuckles. I scratched underneath her ears.

❝Poor thing... you must be lost. Someone must miss you very much. ❞

"Poor thing," I said, "you must be lost. Someone must miss you very much."

Carefully I picked up the cat, testing her reaction to being held. To my surprise, she nuzzled my ear underneath my hair and started to purr loudly. I could feel the vibrations interfere with my heartbeat.

"Brian, Carol – come here a second," I called into the corridor. "What's up?" Dark and wiry, Brian walked in the door and got halfway to the desk before he noticed the cat.

"Oh, no. Keep it away from me," he said. He held his hands out in front of him and backed into Carol.

"What a sweetheart!" Carol said when she saw the kitten. I always knew Carol's curly red hair and Earth Mother looks reflected a warm, soft heart.

"Where did you come from?" she cooed at her.

Brian sneezed.

"I found her here on my desk," I said, "eating my danish. One of you two left the back door open."

Brian grimaced in guilt. His eyes were watering and he looked like he was going to sneeze again.

"What are we going to do with her?" I asked them. "She doesn't have a collar, but she has to belong to someone."

"We can put up signs," Carol said.

"Yeah," I said. "And I could put a notice in the paper. But what are we going to do with her until someone comes to get her?"

"Oh, Heather, I can't take her," Carol replied apologetically. "Between the kids and the dogs, we'd have nowhere to keep her. My husband would kill me. And besides, we'd have to keep the other animals separate for a couple of weeks until she got her shots. That would be almost impossible at Christmastime."

"Don't look at me," Brian said, "You can see I'm allergic."

I frowned. "We can't just leave her here."

The kitten had purred herself to sleep, her eyes closed in contentment. I twisted my engagement ring around my finger. "Darn. I'm not supposed to have pets."

"Just put her back outside. She'll find her way home," Brian said.

Carol and I glared at him.

"Hey, just a suggestion," he said.

I watched the sleeping cat and thought of my options. I wouldn't have been able to live with myself if I'd taken her to the pound. Thoughts of white-clad veterinarians with death-inducing needles pointed at this small, helpless kitten filled my head.

"Heather," Carol began timidly, "have you considered that someone might have just left the cat in the park? I mean, she DOES look pretty hungry, she doesn't have a collar, and there aren't many residential areas around here."

"Why would anyone abandon such a sweet kitten?" I asked. No one said anything. The fact that we, ourselves, couldn't decide what to do with her answered the question for us.

"All right, I'll take her for tonight. Bill will be furious, but what can I do? I just hope that someone answers one of the posters."

The kitten was very small and so well-behaved that I didn't bother trying to find her a cage or a box for the ride home. As I drove, she curled up on my lap. I could hear her purring over the noise of the engine the entire way home.

When I reached my building, I tucked the cat into my elbow, supporting her belly. Her legs dangled on either side of my arm. With one hand, I held her in the crook of my arm while with the other I fumbled with the car door, then my purse for the house keys.

"Darn," I muttered. They always migrated to the bottom of the bag.

At last I had them. I juggled cat and key chain until I managed to get the correct key pointed in the general direction of the door.

"Heather," Bill said from behind me, "you're home." I dropped the keys. The cat yawned.

"Bill. Hey! How was your day?" I tried to sound casual.

He bent down to retrieve my keys. I shifted the cat to my other arm. Back on his feet, Bill took one look at the cat. One eyebrow raised, he kissed my cheek.

"Another neighbor's cat?" he asked. He unlocked the door and pushed it open for me.

I bit my lip. "Not exactly."

Before he could respond, I said, "Bill, it's only for a couple of days, only until I can find her a home."

I set the cat down on the dining room table. The pale, polished wood supported my sole Christmas decoration, the one-foot-tall tree I bought at the hardware store down the street, sparsely decorated with five ornaments, one string of lights and a wobbly star on the highest bough. The skinny tree was already losing its needles.

The kitten sniffed at the green branches and fallen needles, exploring the tabletop domain. She looked over the edge and backed away, content to remain on high perch.

My apartment was small, but tidy. A kitchen and dining area faced the front, and the adjoining living room opened onto a small fenced porch. A narrow flight of stairs led up to the bedroom and bathroom. The white walls were decorated with Chagall prints.

I rummaged through the cupboards until I found the one can of cat food I knew I had somewhere. I opened the can, emptied it into a bowl and put it under the tree in front of the cat. She sniffed it.

Bill stood watching me, his arms crossed across his chest.

"Only a couple of days, eh? Heather, I can't let you keep the cat. If the other tenants found out, they'd be furious. We all signed the same no-pets agreement."

I looked down at the tops of my shoes. They were wet from the melted snow.

"I know. She's just so tiny and helpless. I couldn't just leave her out in the cold, hungry and homeless! For goodness sake, it's Christmas! Where's your Christmas spirit?"

I ranted and fumed. I figured if Bill had to concentrate on calming me down, he would concentrate less on the cat. What's worse, an irate girlfriend or one small cat in her apartment?

"OK, OK," he said finally. "No need to get upset. I suppose you could keep it out on the porch." That was the answer I was looking for.

"Oh that'd be perfect –"

"Just until you find it a home..."

I kissed him. "Thank you, Bill."

He mumbled something about regretting this when it came time to collect the rent.

The kitten was still occupied with her food. I turned on the stereo and put a tape of Christmas music in the tape deck. Bill sat down on the couch. I sat next to him and snuggled into his shoulder, tucking my feet up under me.

"So what should we name her?"

"Who?"

"The kitten, of course."

"Heather, you know you can't keep it."

"Well, we just can't keep calling her 'the cat', can we?"

Bill sighed. Then his face lit up.

"How about 'Chocolate'?"

I frowned. "That's a pretty strange name for a kitten."

"Oh, I don't know. She's dark and she's a temptation that you know you really should stay away from, but you just can't."

I patted his arm. "You have your vices too, you know."

"Here, Chocolate," Bill called. The kitten raised her head from her food and looked at Bill. She licked her face, her pink tongue curling over her whiskers.

"See! She even answers to it!" Bill chuckled. The cat went back to her dish.

"We could call her Tiger or Beauty or Samantha or some-

61

thing," I suggested. No amount of calling got any response from the cat with any of these names.

Bill said, "Looks like she's named herself."

I walked over to the newly named kitten and sighed. I figured I could be generous. It wasn't a bad name, actually, once I thought about it. And after all, Bill WAS letting me keep her here against his better judgment.

"You were hungry, weren't you, Chocolate?" She had nearly finished the whole can of food. I filled the bowl with water. She lapped at it greedily. Saturated, she licked a stray droplet of water off her spotless fur. Her stomach was hugely distended. I wondered how such a little animal could dispose of so much food.

She began to purr.

Carefully, I picked her up and put her on the floor. With her tail raised straight up like a plume of black smoke, she sniffed every inch of the apartment. The mysteries of the kitchen garbage can, the television stand and all the chairs dissipated under her questing whiskers. She looked up the stairs, but didn't try to climb them. I followed her over to the couch.

Bill watched Chocolate intently. She sniffed at his shoes, rubbed up against them, tail still held high, then hopped up onto his lap. She curled up into a ball, wrapped her tail around her body, closed her eyes and began to purr loudly. His eyes softened. I sat down next to him and buried my fingers in the dense fur at her neck.

"Too bad we can't keep her," I said with a smile.

He didn't answer.

When Bill went back to his own apartment, I let Chocolate out onto the porch, where she gravely sniffed every blade of grass. A sparrow nesting in one of the bushes chattered at her angrily, but the kitten just cocked her head and watched the bird. She did her business under the holly bush and scratched dirt over the wet earth. I figured she was house-trained.

Instead of putting her out on the porch, I brought Chocolate upstairs with me. She curled up in the hollow between my neck and my shoulder and slept there all night.

The next morning I woke early and went to the grocery store to buy cat food. Unsure exactly what kind was best for a kitten, I asked the butcher. He pointed to the liver and guaranteed it to be a hit. It was also on sale. Still, it was an expensive habit for a pet, and I made a mental note to ask Carol for some advice about cat food.

Under the watchful eye of a homeless man across the street, I fished an empty cardboard box out of the green dumpster behind the store with the thought of creating a litter box. The weatherman predicted a heavy storm was coming in the next few days, and despite Bill's protests, I didn't want to leave Chocolate out in the cold.

I left the makeshift litter box in the corner of the kitchen, on several sheets of the Sunday newspaper. Chocolate immediately jumped into it and scratched around a bit. Next to the litter

box, I left a bowl of water, and another of dried food. I glanced around the apartment, wondering if she would be all right here alone. I was already late. She was fast asleep in the crack between the cushions of the couch when I raced off to work.

On my lunch break, I made up a flyer. In big black letters, I wrote: "FOUND: Black and brown-striped female kitten, three months old, call 748-0671." Then I made copies and put up as many as I could. I posted some on the billboard at the center of the park and some at the library and grocery store.

I hung the last of my signs on the telephone pole outside the local elementary school. Just as I was doing that the school bell rang. Hundreds of kids ran out of the doors, shouting and laughing. I turned to head back to work. A little girl with pink ribbons in her blonde ponytails stopped to stare wistfully at my sign. A tiny tear rolled down her cheek. I bent to comfort her, to tell her it was all right. She turned and fled. Watching her go, I wondered if it really was.

*T*he storm struck the city practically overnight. Power lines failed under the barrage of lightning, and bridges were closed because of the icy roads. I looked for Inches and Miles, but they remained hidden. Their owners probably kept them safe and warm at home.

Frantically, I tried to find someone to take Chocolate in case her real owner didn't surface. I called every name in my telephone book and spread the word at work. With Christmas coming, and so many little girls wishing for kittens, someone was bound to take her.

If no one claimed her soon, I would have to take her to the Humane Society. And if I couldn't find a home for her, they probably wouldn't be able to, either. I didn't know how long the Humane Society kept animals before they had to put them to sleep. I tried not to think about it.

On Wednesday, Bill invited me to go caroling with some friends. At first, I declined. I didn't want to leave the kitten alone any longer than I had to. And what if someone tried to call?

"Heather, you are spending more time worrying about that cat than you do about yourself," Bill said. "Christmas only comes once a year, you know."

"You're the one that keeps telling me if I don't find a home for her soon, I'll have to take her to the pound. I just want to find her a good home."

Bill grumbled: "You have an answering machine, Heather. I'm taking you out caroling even if I have to drag you out." Arms crossed, he waited for my answer.

"But..."

"Let's go."

I went, but I spent the entire evening worrying about Chocolate. I couldn't help it. What if someone was trying to call, and I wasn't home? Never mind the answering machine. I'm always surprised at people who leave any messages at all; I never do. I wondered about the people living in the brightly lit houses where we sang – whether they had pets, or if they wanted one. If I lived in my own house, nothing would stop me from keeping Chocolate.

I tried to ask the woman at one house if she had lost a cat, but Bill pulled me away before she could answer. As soon as we got home, I checked the answering machine. There were no messages. Chocolate slept under the branches of the Christmas tree like a furry Christmas present.

*O*n Thursday, Bill came around to invite me to a showing of *A Christmas Carol* at the local theater. I resisted, stubbornly determined not to let him drag me away from home. He must have seen the set of my jaw, or maybe he just figured the weather was too bad, because he didn't force the issue. I stayed home and waited for calls.

The weather was getting worse. I stayed home from work on Friday and missed the office Christmas party. Outside, the wind and snow painted the world a swirling and white cold. I sat on the floor, teasing Chocolate with a bedraggled hair ribbon. Like a boxer, up on her hind legs, she batted at it. As I drew it across the carpet, she chased after it. Her eyes dilated, she balanced on her hind legs, pulling her front paws up under her body. At the last second, she shook her hindquarters and pounced.

A couple of people called in response to the ad in the paper. One man had lost a cat nearly twenty miles from here two weeks ago. He just wanted to make sure this kitten couldn't in some way have been mistaken for the five-year-old tom cat he had lost. His voice sounded hopeful, then dejected, then determined.

I asked him if he wanted a new kitten.

"No, thank you. Old Jasper will show up," he said, "It's just a matter of time." The other calls were the same – worried people who instinctively knew this wasn't their cat but who were checking anyway, just to make sure. I answered the phone with a mixture of hope and fear. I was glad they'd called. The calls made me hope that somewhere, someone was also searching frantically for my Chocolate.

But secretly, I hoped that no one claimed her. I knew Bill wouldn't let me keep her, but I fantasized about it.

The television droned. A man in a cheap suit talked about the "horrible storm racking our city." It was the worst since 1985. I wondered if all the signs I had put up were lost under the snow. Come spring, they would surface and some poor cat owner would regret leaving his door open for Chocolate to get out.

The phone rang again. I jumped up to answer it immediately. It was a wrong number.

Then there was a knock on the door. It was Bill. He wore a red turtleneck and black slacks that, despite his tall, thin frame, made him look like Santa Claus. He brushed the snow off his shoulders and out of his hair before coming in. A paper bag of Chinese food protruded from under his arm.

> *But, secretly, I hoped that no one claimed her. I knew Bill wouldn't let me keep her, but I fantasized about it.*

Without a word, he handed me a pair of chopsticks and started removing paper cartons of food onto the kitchen counter. I took a bottle of wine out of the refrigerator.

We ate on the floor in the living room. Bill described the

presents he bought for his family and the crowds at the mall. He talked for a long time about nothing in particular. I listened in silence. It was nice to just listen.

The empty plates and open cartons of food were spread out on the floor in a random pattern. Chocolate sniffed at the empty dishes. They weren't enough to occupy her interest. She returned to her latest find, a dust ball behind the couch.

Bill watched her wobbly kitten movements. "Haven't found her owner yet, I take it?" he asked.

I stared at my hands holding the wine glass. "Not yet."

He looked at me for a few seconds, then nodded and swirled the dark wine around in his glass. The clear liquid reflected the fluorescent light like sunlight on a lake.

On Christmas Eve, Bill and I went to his parents' house for dinner. We drank and stuffed ourselves with food and then talked about what we shouldn't have eaten. Bill's parents asked us about our wedding plans for the spring.

The huge, bright Christmas tree in the living room blinked in front of a window. Outside, it was snowing. Bill's mom had put *Let It Snow, Let It Snow, Let It Snow* on the radio. The whole room looked like a scene from a Christmas card. We exchanged gifts and left early.

I woke late the next morning to a sky of brilliant blue and a layer of pure white snow on the ground. There were tracks and footprints where kids had dragged their new Christmas sleds across it. As fast as the storm had come, it left.

Bill came by and sat down at the table. I brought two mugs of coffee and sat next to him.

"You missed a present, you know," he said. He pointed to a small box under the tree. It hadn't been there the night before. The shape of it looked strangely familiar.

"Well, aren't you going to open it?" he asked. He looked like a little boy waiting for a practical joke to be sprung.

I picked it up and tore the wrapping off the box. It was the

67

green velvet case that had held my engagement ring.

I hesitated before opening it. He looked at me with raised eyebrows as if to say, "Well, go on." The hinges creaked a little as I pried the lid open. There, curled up within the box, was a shiny red collar and a tag that said 'Chocolate' on it.

"Merry Christmas, Heather," Bill said, taking my hand.

"B-b-but, I can't keep her. You said I couldn't keep her. We aren't supposed to have pets..." I sputtered.

"You were so busy baby-sitting and waiting for her owner to call, you missed the homeowners' meeting." Dimly I remembered his asking me if I was going to make the meeting.

"I brought up the subject," Bill continued, "and a number of the tenants wanted pets." I leaned over and kissed him.

He grinned. "Anyway," he said, "now I can raise the rent."

A Buddy for Christmas

By ROBERTA SANDLER

"**H**ow about inviting me in for coffee?" Tom asked, his nose just inches from mine as we stood on my porch. The moonlight cast palm tree shadows across his face. The warm Florida night air was balmy. It was hard to believe it was wintertime, just three days away from Christmas.

"It's not a good idea," I said, holding my door key. "I'm living with somebody. His name is Buddy, and he wouldn't take kindly to my bringing a man into the house."

Tom stiffened. He backed away slightly.

"Oh, I didn't know." He stepped off the porch and made a waving gesture that was more like a salute. "Well, guess I'll see you at work tomorrow. G'night."

I smiled and turned the key in the lock. "Thanks for bringing me home from the Christmas party," I said.

I had left my car at home and gotten a lift to work, knowing I might get caught up in the festivities and have a couple of drinks.

Since Tom lived in my neighborhood, and he didn't drink, I knew he'd be glad to take me home, especially since he had asked me out several times – offers I'd politely refused. Tom was a nice guy, an account executive at the firm where I worked. But I liked Tom as a friend, not as a date. I had no desire to return his romantic feelings.

All I had to do to discourage a man was to tell him about the jealous male I lived with, and how Buddy was so protective of me. It's not that I was lying. It's just that I wasn't telling the whole story.

"Buddy, I'm home," I called out, surprised that he hadn't come to the door to greet me as soon as he heard me enter the house.

But then, Buddy was hard to figure out. Sometimes he was sweetly affectionate, and other times he was aloof, almost withdrawn, as though he were ignoring me. That unpredictability was a quality that I liked in him.

I kicked off my heels and padded barefoot into the kitchen to prepare Buddy's dinner and mine. There he was, impatiently waiting alongside his food dish. He sidled up to me, purring and brushing his long coat against my leg.

"Hi, Buddy," I cooed, kneeling down to stroke his back. "Have you been a good cat? Did you miss me?"

Buddy purred again and peered up at me as if to say, "Can you feed me? I'm hungry."

I laughed and locked the can of cat food inside the jaws of the electric can opener. The can spun around. I emptied the contents into Buddy's bowl, and he eagerly lapped up his meal.

This was one of the best things about being a single, thirty-year-old woman. It was just Buddy and me. No man to have to clean up after or answer to, or to infringe on my freedom and my lifestyle. I came and went as I pleased.

There was no career jealousy between Buddy and me, no disagreements about budgeting money or time, no getting in each other's way or on each other's nerves. I'd had enough of all that when I was married to Warren. Too young and too immature to commit to something as serious as a marriage, we had divorced after eighteen months.

Since then, I'd concentrated completely on my career, and devotion to my work rewarded me with several promotions. It fueled my independence and my pride in being able to manage entirely on my own.

Occasionally I dated, but I was sour on the idea of a long-term relationship. As soon as a man wanted to become serious with me, I shied away. Only at Christmastime did I feel lonely and in need of companionship. It was, after all, a time of togetherness, of families sharing the holidays. But for me, there was no family. I was an only child, and my parents had passed away a few years ago.

Three years earlier, I had decided to adopt a cat from the local animal shelter. A lifelong animal lover, I actually would have preferred to adopt a dog. But I knew that, with my work schedule, I couldn't devote enough time to a dog.

Besides, as soon as I spotted Buddy, I knew this was the pet for me. It was the way he scrutinized me from behind the wire cage. He regarded me thoughtfully, as though he were considering me, rather than the other way around.

"Well, do I measure up to your standards?" I had whispered to him. At first, Buddy did nothing but stare. Then, he cautiously stuck his nose through the cage and purred. It was a short, low purr, but I interpreted it as a simple "yes" from a feline who knew his mind and had no time for pussy-footing around, so to speak.

"Thank you, little buddy," I told him. "You win my approval, too." I had addressed him as 'buddy', meaning it in general terms, not as a proper name, but as he rode home with me in my car, attentively gazing up at me, and being careful not to reward me too quickly with his affections, I realized that Buddy was the perfect name. That was just what he was going to be.

The woman at the animal shelter didn't have much information about Buddy, other than that he had been a stray cat wandering the streets, sifting through garbage.

No one knew whether he had ever belonged to anyone, and his independent, guarded manner toward humans led me to believe that he had been a streetwise cat for a long time.

Buddy would freeze when I patted him, as if he were uncertain about whether I was about to harm him. The sometimes harsh, uncaring outside world had not prepared him for the loving, sheltered inside world I was offering him.

In the beginning, he would never come to me when I called. He would approach only on his own terms, at his own will, sometimes when I was watching TV, sometimes when I was in the midst of a household task.

> *❛Buddy would freeze when I patted him, as if he were uncertain about whether I was about to harm him.❜*

He'd brush against my arm or my leg. He'd sometimes wrap his furry tail around my leg. Other times, he'd stick his face right up against mine, stare at me with wide marble eyes, and sing a purring song – but only when he felt like it.

Until, that is, the night I casually asked him, "Hey, are you my good Buddy?"

From the chair across from mine, Buddy contemplated my question. Then he dashed across the floor and up into my arms, where he cuddled contentedly, a happy purr vibrating throughout his body.

To Buddy, I suppose, "Are you my good Buddy?" translated into "Do you love me?" and that dependable response, where he'd jump into my arms, became his reply of "Yes, I love you, and I know that you love me."

We were a team, Buddy and I. Whatever unhappiness or loneliness we had experienced before we met had dissolved, replaced by a mutual appreciation and closeness. I grew so attached to Buddy that I could not imagine life without him.

*O*utside, the sky was midnight blue and dotted with shimmering stars. Birds-of-paradise and other flowers bloomed against the wooden fence, sharing backyard space with a dwarf banana tree and two fruit trees.

In the middle of the yard, there was a graceful queen palm tree, its fronds waving up and down in the breeze, like the delicate arms of ballerinas. More than any other feature of the house, the beautiful palm tree, so representative of the Southern landscape, enticed me to put in a bid when the real estate agent guided me through the house.

I loved living in Florida. I grew up here. The only thing I found lacking was the snow that was so integral to the Christmas season. Christmas was almost a 'pretend' holiday in Florida, where the occasion was often heralded by hot weather, humidity and swimsuit-clad tourists.

The only semblance of reality was the Christmas tree I purchased and decorated each winter. At the foot of the tree, I'd place gaily gift-wrapped packages, meant for a few dear friends and two sweet neighborhood children who adored Buddy.

On Christmas afternoon, these children would come by for milk and cookies and the token presents that awaited them under my tree. My friends would drop by for eggnog and to exchange gifts. Also under the tree, there was always a present for Buddy, usually some kind of toy.

This, then, was the ritual of Christmas Day, and, for three years, I took it for granted that Buddy would share it with me. However, after one fateful Christmas, I never took the day for granted again.

Two nights before Christmas that year, I opened the sliding door that led out to my backyard. As usual, Buddy scampered outside. My custom was to go back into the house while Buddy took care of his needs, then let him back inside.

> *❝I took it for granted that Buddy would share Christmas with me. However, I never took that day for granted again.❞*

That night, I remained out in the yard, even though it was quite dark and just past midnight. Guided by the light of the moonlight, I stepped over to the banana tree to see how the bunches were growing. I couldn't see where Buddy had gone. Darn. I keep forgetting to replace that bulb, I chastised myself as I looked up toward the patio fixture.

I heard a rustling noise in the grass.

"Buddy, is that you?" I called out. "Come on, Buddy, let's go back inside."

There was silence. Except for the light swaying of the palm fronds and the chirping of a cricket, the night was still. Then I heard the sound again. It was coming from the grass. I moved closer to the sound and bent forward a bit.

"There you are, Buddy," I said, recognizing the shape of my cat. "Come on inside."

Buddy's back lifted into the air. He hissed angrily. I blinked. He was hissing at something in the grass a few feet away. It was sort of rounded. It must be some kind of animal, I thought. It had what appeared to be a pattern on its back. Like a tortoise.

Where I lived, in a rural country setting surrounded by forest, it wasn't unusual to find a wayward tortoise on my property. Once I had spotted a ferret in my yard, and another time I came upon an armadillo who, upon seeing me, hurried away, its armored shell seeming to weigh heavily on its back.

"Oh, it's a big old turtle," I said aloud, as if Buddy could understand me. It wasn't moving. Maybe it was injured. That thought upset me. I didn't know anything about turtles, but maybe there was something I could do to help it.

I left Buddy standing guard over the tortoise while I hurried back into the house. From the pantry closet, I took a flashlight.

I ambled back out to the grass beyond the patio, the flashlight aimed toward the tortoise a few feet from Buddy. My cat was still at his post, hissing for all he was worth.

"It's OK, Buddy," I told him. I figured he was upset because the tortoise was an intruder upon our property.

The flashlight flickered. I shook it. It went out. It came on again, but weakly. That made it difficult for me to distinguish the condition of the tortoise.

The tortoise made a noise. A strange noise. I didn't know that turtles could sound like that. It was a kind of a vibrating noise. No. Not exactly vibrating. More like...

I bent down for a closer look. The bulb inside the flashlight brightened. Now I could clearly see. I gasped. Oh, no. What had seemed like a round shell was now uncoiled skin, leading up to a long-necked, serpentine face.

And the noise...not a vibration. It was a rattle. My heart started beating as though it had been stung with a syringe full of adrenaline. This was no turtle. It was, in its uncurled

75

length, a monstrous rattlesnake.

"Oh, my God," I blurted out, half frozen in my tracks, half urging myself to get out of the way as the snake's tongue darted out. I was so shocked, so frightened, that my feet may as well have been glued to the ground. The serpent, ugly and dangerous as it was, was fascinating.

Here, in front of me, ready to lunge at me in the darkness of that December night, was the face of an angry, hostile snake, on the verge of attack. It rattled again loudly.

I don't know if I could have gotten out of harm's way fast enough. I do know that suddenly Buddy dove in front of me – as though the cat were shielding me – and at that instant, the snake lunged forward, its fangs sinking into Buddy's face.

I screamed. Triumphant, the snake slithered away under the fence. Buddy lay on his side on the grass. He was panting. There was blood above his eye.

"It's OK, my sweet little buddy," I sobbed, stroking his little body. I knew I had to act quickly and lucidly, although my eyes were blinded by bitter tears.

I nearly tripped on the patio ledge as I ran back into the

house. I pulled so hard on the kitchen drawer that it came off its rollers and landed on the floor, the contents spilling out.

The drawer was where I kept my address book. The floral design cover peered up at me. I grabbed the book and flipped through it until I came upon the V page – Veterinarian. My tears fell onto the page.

Buddy was a healthy cat, so except for his yearly inoculations, I had no reason to take him to the vet. It had been a while since I had been there. I dialed the number, expecting to be connected with an answering service because it was now past midnight.

"Dr. Harrison," came the voice from the other end. First, I was surprised that anyone would answer the phone at this hour of night. Second, I didn't know a Dr. Harrison. I had been taking Buddy to Dr. Bettman.

"This is Julie Porter. My cat Buddy has just been bitten by a rattlesnake. Please, can you help me? It's an emergency."

My words spilled out so desperately that I could hear the quiver in my voice.

"Can you identify the snake?" Dr. Harrison asked.

I didn't know what kind it was, but I did remember its colors. I tried to speak calmly, so that I wouldn't have to repeat myself.

"It had a black face, and its body was patterned with black and brown colors, I think."

Dr. Harrison grunted.

"It must have been a rattlesnake. They can be deadly. I'm sending my assistant over to the hospital for a serum to fight the venom. Meanwhile, give me your address. I've got a mobile emergency van and I can be there in five minutes."

Horrified by Dr. Harrison's use of the word 'deadly', yet relieved that help was on its way, I gave him directions. When I hung up, I grabbed the afghan blanket draped over the back of my couch and raced to Buddy to cover him with it.

Buddy's eye was puffed, and his face had begun to swell. He whimpered. I kept patting his back and trying to soothe him with encouraging words. He looked so helpless.

With the back of my hand, I wiped away the tears that wouldn't stop. How could this have happened? This was the Christmas season. This was a happy time.

I looked up at the sky, a big, benevolent dark canopy covering the world below.

"Please God, don't let Buddy die," I whispered.

Mercifully, only a few minutes passed before I heard the sound of a vehicle pulling into the drive, which led to the garage at the side of my house. The garage was just in front of the side yard. I ran to the gate and motioned for Dr. Harrison to follow me.

> ❝ *Please God, don't let Buddy die.* ❞

He knelt down in front of Buddy.

"It's OK, fella," Dr. Harrison said soothingly. But I knew from his frown that he was concerned about the ugly way Buddy's face had swelled.

"I'm going to place your cat on fluid and sedate him a bit," Dr. Harrison told me, preparing a needle. "I'm also treating him for shock so I can transport him more easily."

I nodded. The veterinarian gingerly picked up Buddy and swathed him in the blanket. He carried him to the van.

"Where is Dr. Bettman?" I asked.

Moving to the driver's side of the van, he said, "Dr. Bettman retired four months ago. I bought the practice from him." He shot a glance at me. "Don't worry. I'm young, but I'm competent."

I was embarrassed. "I'm sorry. It's just that I've never seen you before." He nodded and hopped up into the van.

"Will Buddy be all right?" I asked.

Dr. Harrison shrugged as he turned the key in the ignition. "I'll do everything I can to save him, Mrs. Porter."

"Miss," I corrected him. "Julie."

"Give me a call or come by later in the morning," he instructed. Then he backed out of the driveway.

It wasn't until an hour later, when I tossed uneasily in my bed, that I lingered on the memory of Dr. Harrison's face. It was a handsome face, with a square jaw and sensitive dark brown eyes framed by slightly long, dark wavy hair.

I turned onto my side and wondered why I was thinking about a man at a time when Buddy was hovering between life and death. I slept fitfully and felt drugged by the time my alarm clock jolted me awake.

First, I telephoned my office and explained why I wouldn't be coming into work. Nettie, the receptionist, was audibly upset when I told her what had happened to Buddy. She said she would say a prayer for Buddy.

It wasn't enough for me to talk to Dr. Harrison on the phone. I intended to go to the animal clinic and to speak with him directly. I also wanted to see Buddy for myself. Surely, my cat was frightened and confused, and I wanted to be with him, to comfort him and tell him I loved him.

When I pulled into the parking lot of the clinic, I noticed a sign that hadn't been there before. Open 24 hours/weekdays. Saturdays, 8 a.m. to noon.

Dr. Bettman had been available only during regular weekday hours, I recalled. It had irked me that I had had to take time off from work to bring Buddy for his checkups.

"Can I help you?" the receptionist asked with a smile.

"My cat was brought here as an emergency case last night," I explained. "I'd like to see him and to talk to Dr. Harrison. My name is Julie Porter."

The woman nodded. I guessed her to be around my age. Pretty. Blonde hair tied loosely in a ribbon at the nape of her neck. She picked up the phone to summon Dr. Harrison.

"Dale, there's a Miss Porter here...about her cat." She placed the phone back on the receiver. "He'll be with you in a minute," she said sweetly.

"Are you new here?" I asked. "You don't look familiar."

She nodded. "Yes, there have been a lot of changes here since Dale took over the practice. I'm Laura Harrison."

Harrison. She was obviously Dr. Harrison's wife. Funny. It shouldn't have mattered, yet I felt a twinge of disappointment. Dr. Dale Harrison was married.

"I'm Dr. Harrison's sister-in-law," she continued. The surprise must have been evident on my face.

She laughed. "A lot of people get confused because Dale and I share the same last name, but that's because I'm married to Dale's brother Ernie. They share the practice."

I glanced down at the business cards in the little plastic holder on top of the receptionist's counter. Dr. Ernest Harrison, DVM, and Dr. Dale Harrison, DVM.

"With Dale and Ernie taking shifts, we're able to keep the clinic open all night," Laura Harrison said. I was about to tell her how grateful I was that her brother-in-law responded so quickly to my emergency, when Dr. Dale Harrison opened the door that led to the waiting area.

"How are you?" he asked politely, yet with genuine concern.

I brushed my hair away from my eye. Suddenly, I wished I had put on makeup.

"I'm OK," I said. "I want to see Buddy. Is he all right?"

Dr. Harrison asked me to follow him. He led me to his office. It was like a regular medical doctor's office, except that there were paintings and photographs of animals everywhere and shelves that held statuettes of dogs and cats.

Dr. Harrison motioned for me to sit down in the chair opposite his desk. He didn't sit behind his desk. Rather, he sat on the edge of his desk, so that his long legs dangled down. I noticed his hands. Strong. Masculine. Hands that I hoped

80

were skilled enough to save my cat.

"Miss Porter...Julie...I'm not going to let you see Buddy for a while."

I protested, but Dr. Harrison put up his hand.

"Let me explain," he said calmly. "Buddy was bitten right over his eye. His head is blown up to twice its normal size. The edema from the top of his skull literally started folding over the front of his head by the time I got him here.

"It's as though somebody were pumping him up with an air hose. I've been watching him go in and out of consciousness. I stayed up with him all night."

"But why can't I see him?" I asked.

Dr. Harrison sighed. "I've flushed and drained the wounds. I gave Buddy a serum to fight the venom, and his response has been favorable. But he's going to have a long haul."

Dr. Harrison stood up and began to pace the office.

> ❛*I've flushed and drained the wounds. I gave Buddy a serum to fight the venom...*❜

"One of the biggest problems with snakebites is that the concentration of venom in the affected areas can be so devastating that the tissue dies. Buddy may end up unable to blink or move his eye because there was some venom injected into his eye. I'm continuing to apply medication to his eye, and I hope it will help."

I felt the tears again. I was embarrassed, but I couldn't help myself. I wanted so desperately to hold my cat.

Dr. Harrison leaned over and put his hand on my arm.

"Don't worry," he said gently. "I'll do everything I can to save Buddy. I know how much he means to you. But right now I don't want him to see you. I want him to remain as rested and calm as possible. No excitement."

I reached into my bag for a tissue and dabbed my eyes.

"He's all I have in the whole world," I sputtered. Oh, it was useless to explain. How could he understand? He had a family. He probably had a girlfriend, too. What would he know about loneliness and the need to be loved?

Dr. Harrison took my hands to help me up from the chair. He escorted me to the waiting room, opened the door and walked me to my car.

"I understand how much Buddy means to you," he said. "In a world where you often can't entrust people with your feelings, a pet will never betray you."

As I leaned against the car, I looked into Dr. Harrison's eyes. There was hurt there. Something...someone had hurt him. I sensed that he found loyalty only in the animals he cared for. I felt a bond of understanding.

He had taken my hand in his, a comforting gesture, I supposed. I squeezed his hand.

"Thank you, Dr. Harrison," I said. He grinned. I noticed how his eyes sort of crinkled. It was a nice touch.

"Julie," he replied, "Call me Dale."

By the time I got home, I was so curious about Dale Harrison that I telephoned my neighbor Molly, who had long ago introduced me to the animal clinic. Molly seemed to know everything about everyone, and what she didn't know, she had ways of finding out.

"Nice man, that Dr. Harrison," she confirmed. "I heard his fiancee broke their engagement and ran off with somebody else. Jilted him. Now, he's married to his work."

"How do you know all this?" I asked.

Molly laughed. "You'd be amazed what you learn from women sitting next to you in a hair salon, especially when one of the women works in the same office as the person you're gossiping about."

By the time I said goodbye to Molly, I felt better, not only about

Buddy's prognosis, but also about the fact that Dale Harrison was an eligible bachelor. Was I simply grateful, or was I attracted to him?

It was probably a moot point. Surely, Dale Harrison had no interest in me. People who have been burned don't usually want to strike more matches.

It was Christmas Eve. Without Buddy to cuddle up with, I felt the intensity of my aloneness. I drove over to the church. I hadn't attended in a long time. Too long. As soon as I stepped inside, I was flooded with a great feeling of peace.

I knelt. I prayed. I prayed for Buddy to be well. I prayed for God to bless Dale Harrison for being a good person. And as tears spilled down my cheeks, I prayed for love. For the world. And for me.

*O*n Christmas Day, my house was terribly silent. No snow outside. No carolers. No sleigh bells. There was a painful artificiality about the holiday as I glanced out the window behind my fake Christmas tree and saw the palm trees in the bright, hot sun.

I didn't expect the neighborhood children to arrive for hours, so I was surprised when my doorbell rang. Maybe it was one of the neighbors, offering sympathies and inquiring about Buddy's condition. The whole neighborhood knew about Buddy.

Dale Harrison stood outside my front door, laughing at my surprised expression.

"I hope I'm not intruding," he said.

"Not at all," I assured him. "Please come in." He stepped into the entrance hallway and smiled down at me.

"Buddy is going to pull through," he said.

Gasping with relief, I threw my arms around him.

I didn't realize the forwardness of my action until I felt Dale's arms enfold me tightly. Then, he put his palm to the back of my hair. I closed my eyes. We lingered that way for several seconds, until his self-consciousness seemed to match mine, and we unlocked ourselves from the embrace.

"Would you like some coffee and cake?" I offered. He nodded. I led him to the dining room table.

As I poured coffee into his mug, Dale said, "The swelling is disappearing. And Buddy's eye is open now. We've been giving him warm compresses and moving him around a lot, and it's working. He's eating, too."

"How soon can I take Buddy home?" I asked eagerly.

"In a few days," Dale answered. "He's a strong cat, but I think he held on because he knows someone loves him."

I swallowed hard. "He saved my life by getting between that snake and me. That's love. And then his life was saved by someone full of love for animals."

Dale sipped at his coffee. The mug camouflaged most of his face, but I could see his dark soulful eyes, filled with affection. And longing. I knew it was the same longing I felt.

I thought about the prayers I had said on Christmas Eve in that little palm tree-shrouded church. I marveled at the possibilities that life has in store for those who are willing to believe, and to trust.

"I guess there isn't anything as powerful...or as important, as love," he said, placing the empty mug on the coffee table with a gentle smile.

"I guess not," I said, smiling back. I had a feeling he was talking about more than my cat.

One of Our Pussycats Is Missing

By SAM & KAROL EWING

Missy, the roly-poly little cat with the soft gray and white fur, was very excited. She raced through the icy streets to see her neighbor and friend, Samantha, the Siamese.

Samantha was sitting on her front porch. She was enjoying the few warm rays of the sun.

"Orange Thing has disappeared!" Missy cried in her high-pitched voice. "She's gone, Samantha! Gone!"

Samantha studied her visitor with her blue Siamese eyes.

"How do you know Orange Thing has disappeared, Missy?" she asked at last.

"Everyone is saying it," Missy answered. Then she added: "Orange Thing's folks have been looking for her all over town. They can't find Orange Thing anywhere! And it's supposed to snow tomorrow! They feel awful. Just awful."

Now, Samantha was an old cat and very wise. Animals often came to her to solve problems. Just as Missy was doing.

"Where can Orange Thing be?" Missy asked.

Missy and Samantha were talking about a beautiful, fluffy cat who was popular with everyone. Orange Thing lived in a house across the street from Samantha. She was a good-hearted cat. She willingly shared her food with any hungry animal that came to her home. She got her name because of her orange fur.

"How long has Orange Thing been missing?" Samantha asked Missy.

"More than a week, Samantha," Missy said. "It's just terrible! And it's supposed to snow tomorrow! Do you think someone could have STOLEN her?" Missy was close to tears.

"Orange Thing is the kind of sweet pussycat some people would catnap," Samantha said. "Bad Jake, the animal catcher, may have taken her away. He's always looking to capture cats and dogs and put them in the animal shelter. But perhaps there's some other reason she can't be found."

"Oh, dear, I do hope we can find her," Missy cried.

"We must search for Orange Thing," Samantha declared. "I want you to find Mr. Bozo and bring him to me. Mr. Bozo knows everyone in this part of town. He can help us."

"I'll find Mr. Bozo right away," Missy said.

Missy hurried from the house. She ran down the alley as fast as her legs could carry her.

Missy wasn't exactly sure where to find Mr. Bozo. He moved around a lot. But she knew many of his special places.

Mr. Bozo's home was a wooden box filled with old clothing. The box was on the back porch of the house where Samantha and her people lived. But Mr. Bozo hadn't been in his box all day.

Because Mr. Bozo didn't live in a house, he was called an

'outside cat'. Because Samantha lived inside the house, she was called a 'house cat'.

Mr. Bozo's daily search for adventure and new friends took him many blocks away from home. He was clever at getting people to give him food. He knew that if he brushed against a cat lover's legs while meowing, they would feed him. One nice lady even mixed an egg in milk to please him.

"People love it when you say 'thank you' with a purr," Mr. Bozo always said. While she searched for Mr. Bozo, Missy kept an eye out for Bad Jake, the animal catcher.

When Missy finally found Mr. Bozo, he was sleeping, curled up to keep warm under a bush four blocks from Samantha's house.

Mr. Bozo was handsome. He was a very large, gray-striped tomcat. He had a white shirt front, white paws and long whiskers that sprang out of his huge head like porcupine quills. Mr. Bozo had scars on his body from arguments with other tomcats.

"Wake up, Mr. Bozo! Wake Up!" Missy cried. "We need you!"

Yawning, Mr. Bozo opened one green eye at a time. He gave his bib a lick with his long, rough tongue and ran a paw over his face.

"What is it, Missy?" Mr. Bozo asked.

"It's awful, Mr. Bozo! Orange Thing is missing. Samantha wants to see you right away. Right away!" Missy repeated.

Mr. Bozo washed his face very carefully with his right paw. Then he stretched, yawned again and pulled himself to his feet.

"OK, Missy," he said. "Let's go."

Mr. Bozo looked up and down the street. He had heard that Bad Jake, the mean animal catcher, was on the prowl for dogs and cats without collars. Mr. Bozo didn't wear one.

With Missy beside him, Mr. Bozo swaggered down the quiet street. The two cats startled some pigeons who were scratching for food.

Samantha the Siamese was waiting patiently on her front porch when Mr. Bozo and Missy arrived.

As usual, Mr. Bozo was charmed by Samantha's appearance. She was so elegant and smart.

"Hello, Miss Samantha," Mr. Bozo meowed. "Missy says you wish to see me."

"Correct, sir," Samantha purred. "We have an important job. We've got to find Orange Thing."

"Can I help? Is there something important I can do?" Missy asked excitedly.

"There certainly is, dear," Samantha answered. "Orange Thing's folks are very upset. Little Stevie and Kathy are very sad. They miss Orange Thing very much. They like you, Missy. So you should go to their house to visit and play with them. That's very important."

"Oh, good!" Missy cried. "I'll do that right away!"

And the little gray and white cat scurried to the Barker home. Soon she was playing with the two children, running and hiding and doing funny things that made them laugh.

Turning her blue eyes on Mr. Bozo, Samantha said, "There are things you must do to find Orange Thing."

Then Samantha told Mr. Bozo his duties.

"Gotcha!" said the tomcat.

"Keep a watchful eye for Bad Jake, the animal catcher," Samantha warned. "He's a terrible man."

"Yes, ma'am," said Mr. Bozo. "I'll be careful."

*T*he moment he left Samantha, Mr. Bozo raced up a pear tree. He went up so fast he didn't stop to sharpen his claws.

"I hope you're not coming up here to get me," Roberta Robin joked. "I just got back into town, you know."

The pretty bird was perched on a tree limb.

"Of course not, Roberta. We're friends," meowed Mr. Bozo. "I've come to ask for help." Mr. Bozo explained to Roberta Robin about the disappearance of Orange Thing.

"I will put an alert on the Tell-A-Bird Telegraph right away," promised the bird. "I'll be in touch with you the moment we get news."

Saying this, Roberta Robin flew to the nearest telephone line. She perched herself on a wire. Using her right foot, she began to tap out a message on the wire.

Click. Click. Click. Click. Click. Click. Roberta's foot spelled out words. Click, click, click.

Birds of all kinds, sitting on telephone lines, heard the urgent message: "DO YOU KNOW WHERE ORANGE THING, THE PUSSYCAT, CAN BE FOUND? IF YOU DO, PLEASE TELL ROBERTA ROBIN."

Roberta Robin repeated the message several times.

Soon birds all over town were asking other birds, "Do you know where Orange Thing, the pussycat, can be found?"

The question spread among robins, sparrows, ravens, starlings, crows and other feathered creatures. The birds passed the message on to the dogs, squirrels, hamsters, cows, horses, cats, rabbits and any other creatures they came upon.

Mr. Bozo continued the serious business of talking to neighborhood pals, asking them about Orange Thing.

Soon he heard loud squawks coming from an open window where Pedro Parrot was perched.

Pedro was a brightly colored bird. He had green, red and yellow feathers and a white beak. Pedro was munching on a mixture of corn, peanuts and sunflower seeds, which he enjoyed very much.

Seeing Mr. Bozo, Pedro let out a loud squawk.

"Hello there, Pedro," Mr. Bozo said.

"Buenos dias, Señor Bozo," the parrot replied. His words meant good day, Mr. Bozo.

Pedro Parrot had come all the way from South America. He spoke only Spanish. But Pedro could understand most animal and bird talk. And Mr. Bozo could understand Pedro.

"I'm trying to find Orange Thing, the pussycat," explained Mr. Bozo. "You know her, don't you?"

"Si," said Pedro, which meant yes.

Pedro helped himself to another mouthful of food.

"She's missing," purred Mr. Bozo. "Have you heard anything about it?"

"Nada," squawked Pedro, swallowing a peanut. The word meant nothing.

"Then I must hurry along," Mr. Bozo said. "If you hear where Orange Thing can be found, will you please get the information to me?"

"Si, señor," Pedro nodded his head.

"So long," Mr. Bozo said, moving on down the street. "And thanks."

"Adios, amigo," said Pedro Parrot. In Spanish, this meant good-bye, friend.

Pedro continued eating his corn, peanuts and sunflower seeds. He let out another loud squawk.

Mr. Bozo told himself that Pedro was a good fellow. Pedro was smart. He would keep his eyes and ears open for news of Orange Thing.

Mr. Bozo looked up and down the street. He kept watching for Bad Jake, the animal catcher.

Sonny and Honey Bunny lived in a fenced-off backyard not far from Squinty Squirrel's tree. Sonny and Honey had five children who were named after the months of the year: Jan, for January, April, May, June and August.

Mr. Bozo hurried up to the happy rabbit family.

90

When Sonny and Honey saw Mr. Bozo coming toward their home, they hopped together to the fence to greet the tomcat.

They both said at the same time:

"Mr. Bozo, how do you do? It's always nice seeing you!"

Sonny and Honey always spoke together. Everything they said rhymed. They were poets. In the neighborhood, they were known as the rhyming rabbits.

"It's nice seeing you, Sonny and Honey," Mr. Bozo said. "But this isn't a social visit. I've come on an important mission."

The Bunnies said together:

"We've heard the news, it's very sad. For Orange Thing, it could be bad."

"Yes," said Mr. Bozo. "I hoped you'd know where she is."

The Bunnies shook their heads and frowned.

"Sorry, dear cat, we don't know that. If we knew, we'd surely tell you."

Then the Bunnies said:

"With you on the job, no one has to worry. We know you'll find that puss in a hurry."

"I hope you're right. I'll keep looking for her," Mr. Bozo said.

He waved his tail at them in a friendly way.

By this time, the five Bunny children had all hopped to the fence. All seven Bunnies sang out together:

"Goodbye, good guy!"

"I have some funny friends," Mr. Bozo told himself. Then he heard the rhyming rabbits call out:

"For heaven's sake, look out for Bad Jake."

Just then a hiss came from a black tomcat behind a wire fence.

The black cat said: "On the prowl are you, Bozo?"

"That's MR. Bozo to you, Napoleon," meowed Mr. Bozo. He fluffed up his striped tail and strutted on. Napoleon didn't like him, he knew. Napoleon was jealous of his popularity.

Mr. Bozo was tempted to stop and challenge Napoleon, but he knew that the search for Orange Thing was more important.

"Bad Jake will probably catch you today," Napoleon shouted after Mr. Bozo. "You don't wear a collar like I do."

"I hope Bad Jake catches you," Napoleon called.

Mr. Bozo didn't answer Napoleon. He clenched his teeth and kept walking.

Just then, Mr. Bozo heard a flutter of wings and the chirping of a bird overhead. Mr. Bozo looked up just as Roberta Robin perched herself on the limb of an apple tree.

"Good news," said Roberta Robin. "We found Orange Thing! Walter Pigeon saw her going into that tool shack on the corner of Seventh and Main. Walter and some other pigeons were there more than a week ago. They were picking at crumbs of food left by the workers.

"Walter Pigeon says the workmen may have locked Orange Thing in the shack by mistake. She was probably asleep."

Mr. Bozo knew work had stopped on a new building at the address Roberta Robin named. He also knew that Orange

Thing was a curious cat who could have gone into the shack.

"Thank you, Roberta, oh, thank you!" said Mr. Bozo. He hurried toward the shack where the workmen had kept supplies. It stood on a large lot.

"Orange Thing! Orange Thing!" Mr. Bozo meowed loudly at the door. "Are you there?"

For a while there was only silence. Then a very weak voice answered: "Is that you, Mr. Bozo?"

It was Orange Thing!

Mr. Bozo's heart beat faster. "Yes. It's Mr. Bozo!" he said excitedly.

Mr. Bozo heard the weak voice of Orange Thing again. "I am so hungry. I am so cold. I need water badly," she meowed.

"Hold on a little longer, pussycat," said Mr. Bozo. "I will soon have you out of there!"

Mr. Bozo studied the door of the shack. It was latched. A metal rod held the door tightly shut.

He leaped at the metal rod. He tried to move it with his paw. Mr. Bozo tried again and again, but each time he failed.

Finally Mr. Bozo sat down. He was exhausted. And he was very upset that he couldn't open the latch.

Mr. Bozo wanted to keep Orange Thing's spirits up.

"Don't worry, Orange Thing," he said. "I'll be right back with someone to help get you out of there."

"Please hurry!" cried Orange Thing.

Actually, Mr. Bozo had no idea how Orange Thing could be set free. He hurried to see Samantha the Siamese. Mr. Bozo knew that if Orange Thing could be freed, Samantha would find a way.

Samantha listened closely as Mr. Bozo told her where Orange Thing was locked up.

Mr. Bozo said, "Only a person can open that door to the shack and free Orange Thing."

"And so someone shall," purred Samantha. "It is almost the time of day when Timmy, that young boy, takes Kozak for his afternoon walk. Go and talk to Kozak about this."

Mr. Bozo pictured Kozak in his mind. Kozak was a gentle dog, white, and very, very big.

Samantha said: "Kozak is much larger and stronger than his young friend, Timmy. He can easily pull Timmy on the leash to the shack to rescue Orange Thing."

"I understand," meowed Mr. Bozo. "I'm on my way."

*M*r. Bozo was in such a rush to talk with Kozak that instead of looking up and down the street as he usually did, Mr. Bozo took a shortcut through an alley toward Kozak's home.

Suddenly Mr. Bozo heard a noise beside him. He heard a whoosh. Something flashed through the air and smacked the ground. It just missed Mr. Bozo. It was a net.

Mr. Bozo quickly ran to the right. He pushed his way in between two large trash cans. He was frightened. His fur stood out. His eyes were large.

When Mr. Bozo raised his head, he saw a huge man with a black beard. The man was holding a long pole with a large net on it. The man was Bad Jake, the animal catcher.

"I've got you now, cat!" snarled Bad Jake. "You are going to the animal shelter."

It was clear to Mr. Bozo that he could not escape. If he ran from between the trash cans, Bad Jake would catch him in the net and take him away.

Mr. Bozo knew he couldn't help Orange Thing if Bad Jake put him in the animal shelter. It was like a prison.

"How can I escape?" Mr. Bozo asked himself. He had no answer. The situation seemed hopeless.

Slowly, Bad Jake came toward Mr. Bozo with the net. The evil grin spread across Bad Jake's face.

Meanwhile, Roberta Robin had been watching Mr. Bozo from the treetops. She saw what Bad Jake was doing. Roberta Robin knew the danger. She flew to the Tell-A-Bird telephone wires. Using her foot, Roberta Robin tapped out another message.

Click. Click. Click, she tapped. "EMERGENCY! ALL BIRDS COME TO SMITH ALLEY IMMEDIATELY!"

In less than a minute, dozens of birds appeared in the air above Bad Jake. There were robins, starlings, sparrows, woodpeckers, hummingbirds and other flying creatures.

"Drive Bad Jake away," Roberta Robin told them. Then she led an attack.

The birds flew at Bad Jake, flapping their wings around his head and pecking at his arms and legs. A small hawk nipped at the seat of Bad Jake's pants. Bad Jake batted at the birds with his net. But there were too many birds all around him. Within seconds, Bad Jake dropped his pole.

Bad Jake ran toward his truck, the birds right behind him. They pecked at his shoulders and back as he ran.

"Go away! Go away!" Bad Jake yelled. He jumped into his truck and drove away as fast as he could.

"I'll never come here again," he called. "That's it! I quit!"

A few seconds later, Mr. Bozo came out from behind the trash cans. "Thank you, birds!" Mr. Bozo meowed.

Mr. Bozo hurried on to Kozak's home. The big dog was lying on his side in his yard. He was a very handsome fellow. He had dark eyes, a dark nose and dark lips. His black collar shimmered against his white, furry body.

When he saw Mr. Bozo, Kozak stood up with his head held high. He had won many prizes in dog shows.

"Hi, Kozak," said Mr. Bozo.

"A good day to you, sir," said the dog.

"Have you heard that Orange Thing, the pussycat, is missing?" asked Mr. Bozo.

"Indeed, I have," sighed the gentleman dog. "A little bird told me. What a shame!" There was true sadness in Kozak's dark eyes.

"Well, I've found her," Mr. Bozo said.

"Oh, how wonderful!" said Kozak, wagging his tail.

"But there's a problem," said Mr. Bozo.

Mr. Bozo explained that the door to the tool shack was closed with the metal rod and that a person had to open it.

Mr. Bozo told Kozak how he was needed to lead his young friend, Timmy, to the shack and save the pussycat.

"Even if your friend doesn't want to go," Mr. Bozo added.

"Oh, dear," barked Kozak. "Timmy will be very upset. Young Timmy won't understand what I'm doing."

Mr. Bozo put a paw on Kozak's shoulder.

"I'm afraid, my friend, this is the only way Orange Thing can be saved," said Mr. Bozo.

"I will do what is best," Kozak said with a sigh. "I hope my young friend, Timmy, will understand."

The rest of the story is history in the neighborhood. Just as Samantha planned, Kozak dragged Timmy to the shack. Kozak began howling and barking and scratching at the shack door.

Timmy, the young boy, wondered why Kozak was acting in such a strange manner. Finally, he opened the door.

Tired, hungry and thirsty, Orange Thing staggered out.

Within minutes, Orange Thing was back with her family. They gave her food and water right away. Then they rushed her to the animal doctor. Luckily, there had been a bit of rainwater and food in the shack. These had kept Orange Thing alive.

It snowed the next day. Orange Thing stayed at home, and Samantha and Missy lay under Samantha's porch.

Samantha said to Missy, "All's well that ends well. But we can all learn an important lesson from this. We must never go into any strange place where we can be locked in. Orange Thing was lucky there was some food and water there. Otherwise..."

Missy had tears in her eyes. "As people say," Missy meowed softly, "curiosity can kill a cat."

"And people, too," Samantha said. "We must all be very careful where we go and what we do."